Testify

Testify

Ms. Michel Moore

www.urbanbooks.net

Urban Books, LLC
300 Farmingdale Road, NY-Route 109
Farmingdale, NY 11735

Testify Copyright © 2018 Ms. Michel Moore

ISBN 13: 978-1-62286-621-2
ISBN 10: 1-62286-621-5

First Trade Paperback Printing January 2018
Printed in the United States of America

10 9 8 7 6 5 4 3 2 1

*This is a work of fiction. Any references or similarities
to actual events, real people, living or dead, or to real
locales are intended to give the novel a sense of reality.
Any similarity in other names, characters, places, and
incidents is entirely coincidental.*

Distributed by Kensington Publishing Corp.
Submit orders to:
Customer Service
400 Hahn Road
Westminster, MD 21157-4627
Phone: 1-800-733-3000
Fax: 1-800-659-2436

Acknowledgments

As I have crafted numerous novels throughout the years, the list of people that support me has grown. My mother, Ella Fletcher and my daughter, author T. C. Littles, have been here to see my visions even when I don't. My husband and rock, author Marlon PS White, holds me down daily and has been since 1999. Major respect and love to all the readers and local folk that stop by my bookstore, Hood Book Headquarters here in Detroit. And lastly, to the Hood Book Ambassadors: you are the greatest book club and moral support a girl could ever have. I salute you all. God bless!

"Revenge is one cold, black-hearted bitch . . .
and then you die! Just like that—done—over!
And so the bullshit begins . . ."

Prologue

I Got the Best Hand

"Come on now, Rev, have some pride about yourself. Be a man about yours like you wanted me to be so damn bad. Boss the fuck up just one time, old man—one freaking time."

"Wait! Wait! Come on now, please, wait! This is a mistake; nothing but a huge misunderstanding between two men. This ain't right, son, it ain't." Easily, you could hear the sound of sheer uncut desperation drag out in each syllable of each word. Praying to God he was anywhere else other than where he was at this very moment, he defensively held up his hands. Taking several deep breaths, he felt his chest heave in and out. It was hard to speak, all things considered, but the reverend pushed through. "Do you know what you doing? You can't, you just can't," he shouted answering his own question.

"Say what? Are you serious, old conniving house nigga," the reply came swift, knowing time was ticking by and the police might show up at any given moment.

"Are you high on something? Wait; put that gun down. Put it down. Please." Once more the overly desperate words rang throughout the entire city block. "Remember, 'vengeance is mine sayeth the Lord.' You need to think about what you're proposing to do, son. This ain't God's way."

"You funny as shit right about now, but it ain't gonna work out for you, playa. Not this time, not today. You official fucked in the game."

"No no no! Hold up! This ain't right," the preacher's bargaining to live to conduct another Sunday service continued. His mouth kept moving, but the words coming out were obviously redundant and falling upon deaf ears.

"Shut the fuck up." The tension grew as the jaws of several people standing around dropped wide open. "Matter of fact, Rev, shut the fuck up before I shut you all the way up. See, I'm a real nigga 24/7 with mines. I don't talk shit and strong-arm motherfuckers. I say what I mean and mean what the fuck I say. So stop begging and negotiating; you done."

There was nothing but tears on both cheeks. With warm stinging piss running down his creased pants leg, Reverend Richards waved his tattered, covered Bible wildly in the air. At this point, he would do and say just about anything to escape his punishment. He showed absolutely no pride. Time for all of that was over. Praying his words would work and the hardened criminal, seasoned thug would show him a small bit of mercy, the reverend continued. "Look, you gotta listen to what I'm saying. Please, I don't deserve this. I'm begging you. It was all just a misunderstanding; a big damn mistake."

"You don't deserve this, huh? Yeah, right. Come on, now, Rev—don't play yourself and don't be standing out in these grimy Detroit streets acting innocent. Begging is out of season around these parts. Correct my black ass if a nigga wrong, but I warned you not to jump out there with me. I done told you I'm one of them motherfuckers that make fools act right whether they want to or not."

"Please, Clay, please. This ain't God's way," the terrified man continued to plead, hoping for a Hail Mary miracle. "Let *him* handle my final judgment. He has the final say."

"God's way—old man, please. I got the final say today; trust that. And would you stop pretending like you give a damn about me and my fucking soul? Keep it a hundred, with your money-hungry ass." Clay's clean-shaven, bald head sweated in the scorching hot summer sun. As his blue jean shorts slightly sagged, showing the upper band of his boxers, his unlaced Tims stayed firmly planted on the curb. Tightly, he held the rubber grip handle of the gun. Strange as it may be, it seemed to be eagerly urging Clay to hurry the hell up and kill the lying son of a bitch standing in front of him taking a cop. "Rev . . . You know you ain't about nothing. And all these weak-minded cowards out here looking at me like I'm half crazy after you done blackmailed them should know the bullshit too. Man of the cloth—yeah, right; you straight foul. I'm surprised somebody ain't been bodied your punk ass."

"Don't do it, son. He ain't worth the bullet," a random voice nonsympathetically shouted from the small group of spell struck spectators. "He'll answer for his sins one day."

"Listen, if you or anybody else don't wanna see this nickel slick Negro pay for what he done did, then I suggest y'all go home—'cause today is his fucking day," he responded after hawking a huge glob of spit in his soon-to-be victim's face. Clay wasn't in the mood for any interference of what he planned on doing. He was 100 percent official with his. Raised in the streets, he couldn't be easily manipulated. He wouldn't be conned by "the Word," like so many others in the uncompassionate crowd the preacher had "worked his magic on" in the past had been. The blank, dark expression in the youngster's stare told it all. It revealed he could care less about the many potential eyewitnesses that stood idly by. If he caught a murder case, then so be it. It was what it was. Clay was intent on revenge, and today was that day.

Reverend Richards, dry throat, struggled to speak. Short of breath, he grew nauseated. He was sick to his stomach. Panic-stricken, his breakfast and lunch wasted no time reappearing. Gagging from the smell and sight of his own vomit, his heart rate increased. Realizing the local dope boy wasn't trying to hear one of his long drawn out sermons, he hyperventilated. He knew the end was drawing near as the tears flowed from his eyes and snot slid down his jaw. Life in Detroit had never been more real in his fifty-one years of living than it was at this moment. He had never been so terrified. He had never been so regretful of his actions. He wanted to repent for everything wrong he had done or said over the past few decades but knew it was way too much for God to forgive. He wanted to believe a miracle was seconds away, but it had yet to come.

"Son, just listen to me. You gotta listen. Hear me out," Reverend Richards, with hands folded, begged in vain, stalling the inevitable. *Where are the authorities when you need them? What's taking them so long? Why haven't none of these people called the police? God, please help me! Please stop this savage from what he has planned. I know I've been doing wrong and not honoring your Word, but please, Lord. Please save me from this boy's wrath. I can change. Just let help come.* Desperate, he wondered when, and if, the police would show up in time to save his life. "I can switch things up. I can clear up all the confusion that has you so angry. I'm serious. Clay, just let me make a call to my people. Let me call my brother. It was just a huge misunderstanding. I swear," he loudly alleged, begging for his life. "Please, for God's sake—one call."

That was it. It was over, and Clay had heard enough. No more time-outs; no more reprieves; and no more lies of making right all the wrongs he'd done. Fed up with hearing the man beg, Clay let one round off. His aim was dead-on. Striking the so-called man of the cloth directly in the left kneecap, stunned neighbors covered their ears to deaden the sound. The good reverend dropped his Bible. From that point on, it was as if everything were moving in slow motion. In agony, not able to stand, the constantly scheming preacher collapsed onto the pavement. His head just missed slamming into the edge of the litter-filled curb. With an immediate gush of dark-colored blood quickly leaking through Reverend Richards's dress pants, one elderly woman looked away while strangely, another person wickedly smirked with satisfaction.

Slowly walking up on the now-sobbing pastor, Clay didn't smile. He didn't frown or show any real true sentiment about what he'd just done or was about to do. This was a part of street life to him; revenge on his enemy when need be. Towering over the cowardly older man, Clay finally sneered with contempt. With his gun still held tightly in one hand, he made use of the other. Ruthlessly, he snatched the gold chain and diamond cross from the wounded man's neck, letting it fall to the ground. Clay was hell-bent on what had to come next. *God can't save your ass this time. You done fucked over way too many motherfuckers.* Still showing no emotion or regret, Clay coldly placed the muzzle of his pistol to the trembling, corrupt preacher's wrinkled forehead. As the small crowd of neighbors watched in disbelief . . . but oddly content, Clay taunted his moaning prey one final time.

"You fake hypocrite—you predator. One call. Is that all you need, one more call? Your credibility is like below zero with me," Clay, standing over the man, vengefully mocked his victim, still showing no mercy. His winter-white wife beater showed off every angry, bulging muscle and every ink-carved tattoo. Lifting his right boot, Clay slammed the sole directly into the middle of the older man's chest. "Your days of 'making calls' and 'fixing thangs' around the way are over. Negotiations are over—believe that. You gotsta give another pint or two for all your sins. How about that for God's so-called homeboy?"

"But no—no; wait, wait," the unscrupulous preacher raised one hand upward. In excruciating pain, the other clutched his bloodied, bone-shattered knee. His eyes desperately searched the onlookers he knew so well for compassion but found none. "Don't y'all see this?" he belted out with tears flowing and his voice cracking. "After all the things I've done for each of you—why isn't anybody stopping him?" His weakening tone vibrated with every syllable that passed across his quivering lips. "Oh my God, one of y'all, please, call the police before he shoots me again! I'm begging in Jesus Christ's name, help me."

Reverend Bernard Richards, the head director of West Side Outreach Ministries, lay bleeding to death in the middle of the pothole-filled Detroit street. Residents were stunned but not budging from where they were. Instead, they stood around whispering. Yet strangely, no one bothered to call for help as their once-beloved minister had asked. Not sanctified senior citizen Thelma Gale, who lived in the apartment building on the crime-ridden block. Not nosy Mr. Jessie, the Block Club president, who wanted things to go back to the days of the past. Not Mr. Jessie's constantly depressed wife called for help. Troubled, drug-addicted teacher, Lynn Banks, teenager Abdul and his little sister all had the opportunity to dial 911 on their cells. Hard as it was to believe, they chose not to. Trinity, a young single mother, nonchalantly cleaned underneath her fingernails while she recorded the altercation-soon-to-turn-murder on her Android. It was as if the group was merely watching a movie rather than being firsthand witnesses to a cold-blooded murder about to take place. Nevertheless, none of the preacher's seemingly loyal parishioners who he "supposedly helped" shed a single tear. He was on his own and had to face the music by himself. God was about to call him home . . . or the devil one. Either way it went, Clay was gonna end his life.

"Look at you . . . the all-so-great-and-above-the-laws-of-the-hood Reverend Richards. Out here begging the next dude and the neighborhood people for mercy that you shit over on the regular. Imagine that; you acting like a real pussy right about now. A real little bitch around these parts," Clay grinned, finally feeling a true sense of accomplishment as he went on. "You need to man up 'cause you can't do jack for me or with me no more. That's history."

"No . . . Wait, Clay."

"No, *you* wait. Truth is, playtime is over, fool. You earned each one of these hot motherfuckers you about to get. Time for you to go all the way to damn sleep. I'm tight on you."

"Please, Clay." In denial, the man's eyes grew wider while still holding on to hope, holding on to the notion his wrongdoing was bigger than the game itself.

"Tell the devil I'll see him later. Now, bleed out, bitch nigga." Clay happily let loose another deadly deliberate round.

Squad car sirens were finally blaring in the far distance answering a mysterious "shots fired" call. All the seemingly innocent bystanders scattered, disappearing into their homes. No one wanted to risk getting questioned by the law. No one wanted to get judged for not being the one who had not called the authorities. There was a motionless body outside of their dwellings. It was sprawled in the middle of the street on display, leaking blood from the gaping bullet holes. Peeking out from behind their curtains and front doors, no one truly cared as the county coroner lastly arrived on the scene. Officially pronouncing the good Reverend Richards dead in the middle of the street, his now sheet-covered body was removed. As far as the neighborhood witnesses were concerned, the reverend was just another casualty; another statistic in Detroit's ever-rising homicide rate. However, to the Detroit Police Department, he was the front-runner-to-be-elected mayor's half brother and top priority on the long list of murders to solve. Discovering the true, raw, uncut circumstances that led to a supposedly godly man being laid out in the middle of an open-air, drug-infested street in broad daylight is where they had to start.

Chapter One

It was extremely early. The morning dew was still moist, and a slight breeze stirred in the air. Residents of the once-upon-a-time tight-knit West Side community were just making their way out of their houses and apartments. Monday was Monday, which was traditionally filled with folk dragging in their ass from the weekend. Whether it be trying to nurse a hangover or having had broken up with your significant other . . . It was the worst. The beginning of the week brought a chance for people to either get it all the way right or all the way wrong. Either way, there was no avoiding the flow of life in the hood. Most had to go to work, others to school, and some to doctors' appointments. The UPS man making deliveries, bums begging, and low-income folk standing in line to get free food or other assistance from Reverend Richards was the norm. Whatever the case, on this warm summer day, the neighborhood was starting to take shape. It would soon be full blast, buzzing with everyday trials and tribulations.

No one seemed to be paying much attention to the everyday goings-on, but as the old saying goes, everyone is being watched even if they don't realize it. Every shut eye ain't closed, and it's never any secrets in the heart of the ghetto. The streets stay talking and slow gathering information low key on the regular. However, at one particularly dilapidated two-family flat located only a few yards down from the church outreach building, it was apparent the block was being eagle-eyed. Clay, the resident dope peddler, was arrogantly standing on the porch. Stretching his tattooed arms upward, he frowned with disdain. He'd been on the block for some time now doing what he did. Which, truth be told, was causing more harm than good. Although he was definitely lining his pockets, he was tearing down the once-tranquil environment. Yet, in his judgmental eyes, he was far from the problem. *People out here straight foolin'. It ain't no way in hell it could be me.* He tugged at his forever-stiff manhood through his dark denim shorts. Staring up the street, he then shook his head. Clay's attitude was one of contempt. Although he could have overlooked his neighbors' daily routines and behavior patterns, he chose not to do so. He stood firmly in judgment. *I wish to hell I would let the next man dictate my cash flow. I'ma ball till the day they bury my black ass. These niggas out here like some worker bees; no pride.*

Growing up basically solo, his demeanor and personality were selfish. Cursed with a single-parent mother who worried herself into an early grave, he'd given up on family respect early on. He never knew fact for sure who his father was. Clay would often think back on several of the men his mother ran with; yet, she said nothing concrete. There had been constant rumors circulating throughout his tumultuous childhood from distant relatives, but never anything proven. Having overheard several of his adult neighbors whisper about his mother's promiscuous tendencies, as a youth, he shrugged it off. He knew he was different than the other kids growing up. Looking in the mirror, Clay easily noticed his skin was extremely lighter than his best friend's and his cousin's. Being teased about his deep waved, so-called good hair had become normal behavior. At various points in his coming of age, he inquired who his dad was, but his mother seemed to have a knack for avoiding that damning conversation of truth. Her repeated response was that her son was God's child, and that was all that mattered. That being said, Clay suffered the ridicule of being labeled "the white man's seed," "half-breed bastard," "pretty boy," and the one he grew to despise the most, "soft-ass nigga with a cut." Walking around with those disparaging remarks looming over his head made Clay a target wherever he went. With no choice whatsoever, the once naïve boy quickly transformed into a bitter, coldhearted teen turning into a hard-core, zero-tolerance monster; one that ruled his crew with an iron fist. Family meant nothing to Clay, and people who had those blood ties amused him. The twice-convicted felon couldn't understand why people were on their porches making such a big deal about telling their kids they loved them or wives shouting for their husbands to have a good day at work. In his crime-filled world, nobody really loved anyone. No one trusted anyone, and what day at work slaving for the next man was really good? Those emotions were reserved for suckers, and he was definitely not classified in that category. As far as he was concerned, the people he was watching were.

Double-checking his fresh wheat-colored Tims for signs of any scuffs, Clay sighed. For some strange reason, he felt it was going to be one of those days that things seemed off in the hood. Not wanting to ever get caught slipping, he pondered switching up the way he moved and the way he thought. It was easy for him to be seen, even if he didn't want to be noticed with the ride he was currently pushing. Police and foes alike knew he was coming a mile away. The game definitely needed a change. Contemplating trading in his leased gas-guzzling Hummer for a low-key vehicle, he rubbed his hand down over his face. Taking one more brief survey of the block,

Clay stepped back into the lower rented flat to make sure everything was running smoothly with his team.

"Yo, what up, doe, Whip? What you think so far? Where we at with it?" He twisted the four deadbolts after slamming the steel-reinforced door closed. "We good or what? What's the deal? Talk to me. What it do? You got a nigga anxious to know."

"Clay, to be honest, my guy, I dunno for sure." Whip reached for the opened box of baking soda. After carefully measuring out a few more teaspoons to the already piping hot Pyrex that was home to the contents of their morning's work, he puzzled. "This play ain't coming back like the other package did yesterday. I don't know what exactly the problem is, but hold tight. I'ma try something else." Bobbing his head to the old-school music that was playing on *The Steve Harvey Morning Show*, he stirred the mixture with the precision of a scientist trying to cure cancer. "If this bullshit here don't do it, we might have to go holler at ole boy. It might just need a little more time and heat. But you know me, playboy, I'm gonna try to make it do what it do."

Clay immediately placed his hand on the handle of his ever-present pistol. Now, garnering a double bad attitude, he stroked the grip, hoping the product he'd just dropped a few Gs on was proper. *Dawg don't wanna see me. Not to-fucking-day of all days. Right about now, I ain't in the mood.* As much as he would try to resist the urge to pop off, he'd fail. Clay stayed in an ongoing battle to remain calm. It was easy to see why, as a child, the doctors suggested some sort of medication for his impromptu rages. But Clay's mother refused. Maybe it was her own demons she was waging battle with where pills were concerned, or just not wanting him to become another labeled "troubled black boy." Just the same, today, as on many other occasions throughout the years,

Clay was seconds away from acting out. If he didn't shake off the feelings of folks being purposely out to get him, he would snap. No one in the small flat wanted that. None of his crew wanted their leader to damn near have to be caged up like some wild animal to get back in his right mind. Thankfully, Clay snapped out of his trance and came back to reality. Watching Whip work his magic with the aid of a few ice cube chips, Clay turned his attention to another pressing matter. Asking his other worker Dorie how things were going on the competition side of the game, Clay's blood pressure rose once more in anticipation of the answer. Having run the streets for years, the game vet knew from experience, even if you had the best dope in the world, some drug addicts would go with the size of the play over quality of the product.

"Yo, Dorie, who out there got a stronger package than us? Who out there making them fucking streets pop off?" Firing off statement after statement, question after question, he waited with sweaty palms, knowing the answer could go either way. "'Cause ya know we need to keep a head banger on they asses. That is, if we wanna eat. You know how picky them motherfuckers can be. We need something that, no matter how big or small, gonna have them beating down the block."

"Well, ole boy an' 'em across Twelfth Street sack is weak as a baby aspirin. It ain't hitting up on much of nothing. But other dude and his soft bread clique tried to come up on some work they supposedly copped from one of them sand niggas near Seven Mile and Woodward." Dorie continued to divulge what he knew while counting money, placing a red rubber band around every stack. "My boy said it was off the hook the first part of the day. They was making all the bread, but by nightfall, they must've cut the dog shit out of it. They flow slowed all the way down, and we came through like a champ and made that late-night rush ours."

"Oh yeah? Real talk? So the count was still good?"

"Yeah, don't worry, Clay. It ain't mess with our bump, though!" He continued to count the assorted bills while making sure all the faces on the bills were in the same direction. "We on top of it out in them streets. You know we always gonna have the best hand; do or die."

"Dig that. Real rap, nine outta ten, they probably can't get no more, so they stretched it." Clay walked over closer to Whip, who was just bringing the massive misshaped boulder together. He grinned, putting a toothpick in his mouth, seeing Whip finally pour "the hardened work" out onto the paper towel-covered plate. "But if this hookup right here is half as good as it was straight up uncut with nothing on it, them heads gonna be dancing in the motherfucking streets; some old *Dancing With The Stars*, Chris Brown dancing shit. Now, one of y'all go get homegirl. We ready to rock and roll and see what's really good with Whip's handiwork," he happily ordered, knowing money was to be made on the floor.

Eight minutes later, an already Wild Irish Rose-intoxicated cross-addicted Ida was let inside the cook up house. If anyone was gonna be able to give them an accurate read on the drug, it would be her. She was a seasoned veteran when it came to getting high. Proudly letting it be known she had been getting "half out of her mind" since the early sixties, Ida grinned. As she wrapped her dry, split lips around the transparent pipe, her usually half-closed eyes opened wide as a deer caught in headlights. One short pull, followed by a few long ones, Ida's jaw started to tighten up. With each hard suck on the glass dick the lifelong crackhead and heroin addict took, Clay started to smile, moving his toothpick to the other side of his mouth. The heavy stream of smoke filling the pipe, then disappearing into Ida's surely dark-infested lungs, made Whip sit back, feeling extremely content with his craft. With a huge smile knowing he'd cooked up another perfect package, his reputation as a master chef was secure once more.

"Well, what up, doe? What's the real official deal?" Clay knew the woman old enough to be his grandmother was feeling it by her outward reactions. "Talk to me, Ida. What's the verdict? We good money or not? Let a nigga know something."

Getting herself together, she was out of breath and off balance. After choking five or six good times, Ida made her final "professional smoker decision" on the quality of what she was testing. "Hell, yeah, Clay," she struggled to speak, coughing once more from the effects of the strong blast she'd just been treated to. "This is the best bump I done had in days—maybe weeks." Her veinless swollen hands dropped the hot stem on the table as her eyes bucked twice their normal size, watering up. "Let me hit some more just to make sure. You know, just in case I'm imagining things. I need to make sure this shit ain't playing tricks on my old mind. Gimme one more blast I can do here, right quick."

"Naw, not here, but good lookin' out, Ida. I'll holler at you next go-around. We gotta get the rest of this shit all the way together, then hit the block hard." Clay then instructed Whip to chip their always-reliable test dummy off another tiny-size rock, then send her on her wasted way to spread the word throughout the streets.

"Hold up now. This is it?" Ida bargained, fixing her matted wig that was cocked to the side. "Come on now, baby boy, this can't be it," she slurred, showing all remaining seven of her rotten teeth. "Don't do me like this, Clay. Hook me up, baby boy." Her wig shifted once more. "You owe me that much after all the times I be out here having your back."

"*I* owe *you?* You be out here having my damn back? What in the hell!"

"Yeah, nigga," she brazenly stuck her chest out as if she was waiting to get a medal pinned on her lapel. "Whenever all them people be out in the streets talking about y'all's dope ain't shit, I be saying it is, even when it do be garbage. And when them other dope boys be saying they gonna catch you slippin' and lay you down for good, I don't be thinking they right."

The room grew silent. It was like the quiet before the storm. The awkward dead zone quiet moment when you get caught in a big-ass lie. Everyone knew Clay had zero tolerance when it came to people questioning him, let alone begging. He was the first, the last, and the only word in his organization. When Clay spoke, people listened. Asking for Whip or Dorie's opinion was one thing, but to have them, or any of his lower-level street runners, speak out of turn was another, especially if they were ordered to shut the fuck up. To Clay, shut the fuck up meant just that . . . *shut the fuck up.* So, when Ida, a common drunk and crackhead, had the audacity to not appreciate his generosity, Clay damn near lost it. The fact he was banging Ida's youngest granddaughter Rhonda on the regular the past month still didn't matter. Clay was beyond heated.

"So hold tight. Let me get this bullshit straight. You up here in this motherfucker telling me niggas out in these streets running off at the mouth? Out there disrespecting my name like I'm some sort of bitch-made ho? And you just now found it in your fucked-up mind-set to put me up on that shit? Like you doing me some sort of hellava favor?" Clay was fighting hard not to put his hands on Ida. Every part of him wanted to not only chin check her, but silence her forever. "You crackhead motherfuckers kill me. Y'all out here running around trying to get high and don't realize how serious shit can be. You lucky I got some other shit to deal with right now, so get the fuck on. And, Whip, take that shit back from her."

"Come on, Clay, don't do me like that. Please, I need that hit." With Wild Irish Rose-liquid courage in her system, Ida kept at it, acting like fat meat ain't greasy and her shit ain't stank.

"Ida, you best chill with all that," Dorie advised, knowing what was about to come next if she didn't take heed to his advice.

"Yo, one of y'all get this foul skank outta here before I snap her goddamn neck! Old head or not, she got me twisted. Now I'm done playing around." He waved his hand dismissing her like she was a fly. "And hurry the fuck up doing it before it get ugly."

High as hell, Ida obviously couldn't see the seriousness on Clay's face or hear it in his tone. "Aww, come on with your ole bright-skin ass. I just need a few more pieces for the road, for later. I know you got it like that. My granddaughter told me how y'all been living; eating at restaurants every night." She continued begging, all while being roughly led to the rear door. "Don't do me like this, Clay. We practically family; me and you."

Whip intervened, personally escorting her to the backyard. Practically shoving her out the gated fence, causing her to land dead on her dusty tailbone, he knew she had to be extra high off his mixture. "Damn, Ida, fall the fuck back. Is you on a suicide mission or what? You know how ole boy get down on that bright-skin bullshit. Now, your best bet is to get the hell on. Take a lap or two before he come out here and stump a mud hole in your ass."

Whether she knew it or not, Whip had just done the old woman the ghetto favor of a lifetime. If she would've stayed inside of that flat any longer, working the boss's nerves, old Ida probably would've come up missing.

That's how life was in Detroit. Snitches got killed, haters got checked, loud-talking Negroes selling wolf tickets got them thangs cashed in, and pesky, begging-ass heads, like Ida, got seriously ghost!

Spending close to an hour weighing and bagging product, Clay and his crew were ready to hit the streets. Finally, they were about to post up in his territory. He had fought long and hard to earn the prime drug area that was his now, and would stand strong to keep it, if need be. The fact the police had found several nude dead bodies in the trunks of abandoned cars making the neighborhood hot made no difference to the team. It was what it was. That was life in the hood, and residents and thugs alike had grown accustomed to it. The police could care less if it was a workingman they would jump out and frisk or one of Clay's boys. An arrest was an arrest was their motto. Squad cars and unmarked vehicles would slow cruise when they had the extra manpower just to knock heads. It was as if some cops were doing it for sport, mad that they were losing the war on crime. But Clay knew the police had a job to do, which was try to catch them doing wrong. He also knew he and his homeboys had a job as well, which was not to get caught doing well.

Day after day, the crew would show up and show out doing theirs. They had one mission and one mission only . . . each day they woke up and their feet touched the ground, and that was to get paid by any means. Even when Clay was hauled in for questioning after rumors surfaced of his possible involvement in their gruesome murders, shit didn't stop. And why would it? There was money to be made in the streets—so that was that. Crackheads had to smoke crack. Dopefiends had to shoot up. And alcoholics needed a drink. The hustle and flow of the game didn't cease because he was off the streets. Like breathing, the game was second nature. Clay understood that and lived by that code. His boys were as close as anything he had as family, and they held it down until Clay touched back in the streets. As the three of them drove dirty as hell past the misfortunate people who'd just received free boxes of cheese, butter, and powdered milk behaving like they'd just won the lottery, Whip and Dorie frowned. Both barely in their twenties shook their heads, not yet knowing the true meaning of the struggle of life.

"Damn, it must be tight out here. They at them baskets like they got gold or some shit in 'em," Dorie observed, making sure the old-school Buick Regal he was driving came to a complete stop at the sign.

Whip, the fastest of all three on foot, held the purple and gold Crown Royal drawstring bag with "the work" inside of it, also staring at the chaos that was going on at the church building. "You ain't never lied. It's almost like when we give out testers," he commented while still trying to keep an eye out for Detroit's Finest in case he had to bail from the backseat.

I wish the fuck I would, Clay, toothpick still in mouth, gangster leaned to the side, low-profiled in the passenger seat. As the car pulled off from the stop sign, Clay and Reverend Richards, the ringmaster of the ghetto circus, momentarily locked eyes. It was as if two big, ferocious dogs would come face-to-face on the regular but neither would attack, let alone bark. They would lift their heads as if they were sniffing out each other's strong scent in the air. Showing no change in facial expressions, they nodded, slow acknowledging each other's presence on the congested block. It was no deep dark secret they were cut from two different cloths. The good reverend assumingly stood for everything righteous in Detroit, while Clay held down all that was bad. Nevertheless, the two had some strange mutual respect for each other—just being black men in America.

Only a few short city streets over from where they'd just hooked up at, Dorie swerved the Burgundy rag roof Regal over, taking up his usual two parking spots. The fact one of them was reserved for handicapped parking never seemed to matter to Dorie one bit. As the cautious yet cocky trio exited the vehicle, the blight-infested block seemed to come alive. The few pockets of families that actually still lived on Monterey Avenue were far, few, and in between. But as far as Clay was concerned, that was their loss and his gain. If they didn't like living in the middle of a ground-zero crime zone, they could pack up and move because he and his team were there to stay. Clay was on the block to make money, not friends. He was about that life, even if they weren't.

Disappearing with the "package" inside the stash house where the runners were waiting for their individual sacks, Whip finally came back out joining Dorie and Clay on the stoop where they started their grind of overseeing.

Chapter Two

Lynn Banks

Like clockwork, it was the same routine day in and day out. Not much changed if you were chasing a high and were dope sick. Everything you said, did, or even thought about was ultimately in the pursuit of getting that next blast. Lynn Banks, a middle-aged elementary school-teacher, was definitely not the exception to that golden ghetto rule. With red, yellow, and royal-blue folders filled with homework assignments and several book reports next to her, Ms. Banks, as her students affectionately called her, sat scrunched down in the front seat of her late-model silver Toyota Corolla. Impatiently waiting for Clay and his crew to arrive and set up shop, she let her rough fingertips rub the smooth sides of the burnt edge pipe that always aided her in her pursuit of ecstasy.

What's taking them so long? She pushed the huge, cheap, tinted sunglasses closer to her face. Lynn prayed no one would recognize her through the superdark lenses. *Wow, I'm going to be late again! I hope they're not out. I don't have time to drive somewhere else for a blast probably the size of the rocks they normally have.* Balling up the Outreach Ministries pamphlet on the type of services they offered, she rolled her eyes. Just thinking about the reverend practically shoving it through her open car window as she waited at the red light on the corner of his church she fumed at his random judgment. *I don't need help from him or his people. What I need is to get right. Why don't those boys hurry up and get here?*

Not truly caring if she made it across town to greet her third-grade class when the first bell rang, Lynn wrung her hands together anticipating the strong package that Clay and his crew were infamous for having. She knew she was already on probation with the school board, pending termination for the amount of times she'd been late over the course of the year, but Lynn, once nominated as Detroit Teacher of the Year, ain't give a damn. She was on a mission. And that was to get seriously high before dealing with a group of slow-minded, ill-mannered, "why in the hell didn't you get it the first time and you wouldn't have needed summer school" badass kids.

"Oh my God—finally." She looked over the top rim of her shades watching the Regal pull up. Exhaling, she checked her watch. "I need to hurry up, take care of my business, and leave. Someone should speak to them about being more prompt." Lynn had the nerve to act like the runners she'd buy rocks from every morning were some of her third-graders who constantly needed reprimanding.

Stepping out of the car, her short sleeve button-up blouse and perfectly ironed beige slacks made her stand out from the rest of the dirty addicts that started to gather no sooner than seeing Clay bend the corner. Paranoid, holding a crisp twenty-dollar bill she'd just taken out of the Bank of America ATM near her house, Lynn's lower lip quivered, knowing she was just moments away from smoking. Having several degrees and a good-paying job didn't matter to the runners who were serving customers. As far as they were concerned, she was no better than Ida or any other whore that tricked in the alley or a vacant house for their cop money. When she stepped up, Lynn was just another "head" in line with a few dollars to spend and would be treated as such.

Practically snatching the plastic baggie from the teenage runner's hand, Lynn recklessly bolted across the street.

"Damn, girl. Slow ya roll." She vaguely heard a voice shout out from the stoop after almost callously knocking down an elderly lady on a cane.

Not offering a simple apology or at least a "my bad" to the woman, Lynn hopped into her car. Starting the engine, the educator noticed the gas light flashing, but could care less if she ran out of petro on the freeway. She'd just spent the last of her life savings on a rock. *Oh yeah, this is a nice size just like I knew it would be,* she marveled, keeping her new treasure clenched in her hand. *I just hope it's strong and can get me where I need to be before dealing with these kids.*

Knowing her habit was way out of control, and all her bills, including her mortgage, were beyond past due, McMichael Elementary third-grade teacher, Lynn Banks, fumbled with a homemade pipe and the red cigarette lighter she kept tucked in the side compartment of her bootleg designer purse. Ripping the baggie open with her clenched teeth, she spit the top down on the floor mat. *Damn, I needed this.* Adjusting the flame as high as it could go, Lynn blazed up the stone. *Yesssssss!* She inhaled, holding the smoke in, and then slowly exhaled. After a few more strong pulls, Lynn let the torch go out as her body collapsed in the seat. Letting the effects of the crack cocaine do what it often did, fuck up a Negro's life, Lynn's mind was cloudy. *Oh my God! This is better than yesterday's . . . way better!* As Lynn took her first pull off the drug that she'd grown to worship, her mind flashed back to happier times before she was crack's number one bottom bitch.

***

"We would like all of our graduates to please stand. Your instructors, the staff along with your family and friends, would like to congratulate you all on obtaining your degrees. Whereas some of you will opt to go even further in your education, others have already been offered positions in your desired field of study."

Lynn was ecstatic as she did as requested by the master of ceremonies. As she stood shoulder to shoulder with her classmates, a strong sense of pride overcame her. Growing up was never a true hardship as most of the youth in Detroit had encountered, but nevertheless, she had obstacles to endure. Born with a speech impediment, Lynn was oftentimes teased. When excited or unsure of a situation, the only child would stutter. In an attempt to help their child flourish, Lynn's parents took her to see all sorts of specialists. But none could help. Thankfully, after a few years, she grew out of her handicap, but not before she was left with mental scars. Deciding to immerse herself into reading books and her studies, Lynn became somewhat of a social recluse. After finally finding the courage to move out of her aging parents' home, she got an apartment on campus. It was there that she was befriended by dorm mates who were likeminded. It was her affiliation with them that gave Lynn Banks her first taste of illegal substances.

"Come on, Lynn, try it. I'm telling you, it will have you feeling so freaking good."

Hesitant, Lynn pushed his hand away. She'd never taken more than an extra strength aspirin before, so smoking weed was, and had been, taboo. "No, thank you. I'm good."

"Come on, girl," her other friend urged after taking her turn at lip locking the homegrown bud.

Despite the increasing peer pressure from both, Lynn remained firm in saying no to drugs. She stood strong in her conviction . . . until late one night. Nearing three o'clock, she was awakened by the repeated sound of her cell phone ringing. Without opening her eyes, Lynn extended her arm from beneath the thick beige-colored blanket. As her hand searched around the nightstand for her phone, there was a knock at the door. Still half asleep and confused, Lynn jumped out of the bed. Thinking it was just another student goofing around, she flung the door open ready to do verbal battle for disturbing her rest. Immediately, she realized it was the dorm director. Minutes later, Lynn Banks's calm, drug-free world was turned upside down. Her first cousin had been trying to get in touch with her. The parents who had loved her since birth, took care of her and gave her everything they had—were gone. Just like that. She had just spoken to her mother earlier and her father a few days prior. Now, thanks to a drunk driver that had struck the couple's car when coming back from Bible Study, Lynn was out here by her lonesome.

For days after the heart wrenching double funeral, she was out of it. She couldn't be consoled. Her two best friends finally took matters into their own hands and demanded that she smoke some weed to calm her nerves. Not in the mood or having the strength to fight off their suggestion again, Lynn gave in. Soon, the gateway drug became her escape from the pain of her reality. Refocused and determined to stay in school, she studied and smoked; smoked and studied. When the now-orphaned female obtained one degree, she decided to get another; this one in teaching.

Only months into her first teaching assignment, Lynn was blessed to find a man interested in her. Her life and their life were as complete and as happy as anyone could hope for. Tragically, as life would have it, Lynn's fairy tale was cut short. The love of her life was snatched away. She once again fought depression, but this time around, weed was not strong enough.

Reaching out to her old college roommates for comfort, they turned her on and out on their new drug of choice: crack cocaine. Still trying to maintain a job and keep a roof over her head, Lynn had become a certified closet smoker. One day the teacher would seek out help, but unfortunately for her students that depended on her for guidance and an education, today was definitely not that day. For now, Lynn Banks and her conscience were the only ones that knew her true shame. When she finally drove off, high as three kites, she purposely ignored the hard stares of Reverend Richards who was still passing out literature and food boxes to the needy.

Thelma Gale

Feeling the harsh reality of her age, Thelma Gale, who always joked that she was seventy-five years young, struggled to get out of the thin mattress bed. In between her chronic arthritis and excruciating back spasms, Thelma tried to stay positive as she started her day. Taking a deep breath, she grabbed for her cane. Her legs were definitely not what they used to be, so needing that had become a necessity. With a small bit of struggle, she was now standing up. Shuffling her feet, the old woman, a mother of five grown children, made it to the bathroom. Reaching up in the medicine cabinet, Thelma removed her dentures out of the plastic blue cup where she placed them every evening. After washing her face, the grey-haired Thelma then headed into the kitchen area of her small one-bedroom apartment in hopes to prepare herself breakfast.

Losing her husband at an early age, Thelma still continued to do whatever she had to do to ensure her kids, as ungrateful yet successful as they turned out to be, had decent, carefree lives. Now, despite their achievements and nice-size bank accounts, none of the five came back to the neighborhood to see about Thelma, let alone considered moving her in with them after the family home burnt down. Now, sadly, every morning, as if on schedule, Thelma would try to call each one of her kids and pray one would answer and bless her with at least a minute or two of conversation.

"Hey, baby," Thelma's hand trembled when her eldest picked up . . . undoubtedly by mistake. "I'm so glad you're not busy."

"Oh, Mama, it's you." Rebecca rolled her eyes to the top of the ceiling, mad she hadn't checked her caller ID. "I thought you were the man from the construction company. I'm expecting his call!"

Thelma placed her hot cup of coffee on the table so she could hold the phone with both hands. "Sorry to bother you, Becky, it's just I haven't heard from you in so long. How are the girls doing?"

"Mama, stop calling me Becky. No one calls me that anymore. It sounds so uncouth. Please call me Rebecca," she argued. "Why would you even name me that if you were going to call me something else?"

Apologetic for angering her rude child, Thelma once again asked about her granddaughters. "Well, what about the girls?"

Rebecca, ashamed of where she came from, had her own issues she was battling and could care less if her mother's personal needs were met. That included simple information about her family. "I'll try to call you next week and let them speak to you," she cut the conversation short. "Now, I have got to go!"

Before Thelma could say good-bye or tell Rebecca to kiss the girls for her, the telephone line went dead.

I guess she has a lot to do. Thelma wanted to believe that, even though she knew better. The only thing she could do was shake her head and think back to better days.

"Come on, y'all children, wake up. Wake up now; y'all hear me?" Thelma stood in the doorway insisting the kids get up and get their day started. *"Becky, you go in the bathroom first and get yourself together. Then the rest of y'all take turns behind her, and hurry up. Breakfast is almost ready, and you know that oatmeal ain't right when it sits. I done made both bacon and ham, so like I said, hurry up."*

"Okay, Mommy," Becky answered, fighting to fully open both eyes. *"And don't forget about my presentation today at school. That's why I have to wear my good dress and my matching ribbons."*

"Shut up, dummy. Mommy ain't gonna forget about that stupid program. That's all you been talking about all week; dang," Thelma's son interjected, letting his true feelings be known.

"You shut up, dummy dumb dumb. You just jealous and ugly."

Already tired of all the back-and-forth between the children, she quickly shut it down. "Look-a here now. Stop with all that bickering. I'm just glad y'all's daddy already done left for work because he would give y'all a spanking for that language. Now get up and get ready, like I said."

The kids all did as they were told. Soon, the big hearty breakfast she would prepare daily for her family was consumed and they were out the door. Thelma stood

*in the doorway watching her offspring walk down a
perfectly manicured lawn and flower-lined block, joined
by their classmates also heading to school. Throwing
her hand up to greet a few neighbors on their way to
work, Thelma smiled, content with her life.*

Still in denial how things had ultimately turned out,
the sickly grandmother opened her kitchen cabinets
wanting nothing more than maybe a hot bowl of grits or
some oatmeal to soothe her hunger pains. Yet, knowing it
was nearing the end of the month, Thelma's shelves were
bare. She had to make the decision to buy food for the
entire month or pay for her much-needed medications.
The small amount of extras the low-income woman did
have, she shared with those in her building that were
even less fortunate than her. As she stood there, a look
of sorrow graced her face. Squinting her eyes, it was easy
to focus on the back of the cabinet wall. What should
have been full of can goods, coffee, and other items the
elderly woman desired . . . was not. Her stomach often
would growl, but she had lived through many hard times
growing up and drank hot tea to soothe the hunger pains.
Well, as part of her would love to live high on the hog, she
not once regretted the decision she was often forced to
make. Although food was high on her list, the pills she
consumed daily kept her alive. Some of the medicines
had to be consumed with food, so a pack of noodles
were often split to serve as two meals. Given the choice,
Thelma chose life, living how she had to.

Trying not to be a burden to her grown, well-to-do
children and ask for help, Thelma got dressed, heading
out to see if she could get a charity box of canned goods
before going to her doctor's appointment. It was the only
way she'd be able to make it through to the following

month without starving. Barely making it down the stairs, Thelma narrowly missed getting practically run over by one of the many fiends that predatorily lined her block every morning waiting to get high.

"Damn, girl. Slow ya roll," a voice forcefully yelled out as Thelma's cane was knocked out of her hand.

Grabbing ahold of the steel handrail just before falling to the ground herself, Thelma's blood pressure quickly soared. Suddenly, she was blessed when one of the young dope dealers, seemingly the leader, at least had enough common courtesy and compassion to try to control their almost always disrespectful customers. Even though she opted not to tell him, she was thankful for his act of kindness. Slowly, the grandmother made her way toward the end of the block where she saw Reverend Richards doing what he did best—talk to people about their many problems and hardships. *Good God, I pray he still has food boxes left. I really could use one this week.*

Mr. Jessie

Standing on his front porch, longtime West Side resident and Block Club President Mr. Jessie shook his head while he pretended to sweep. Rubbing his salt-and-pepper-colored beard, he could only think back to the good old days. The ones when his neighborhood, in particular, his own block, was filled with well maintained homes and other hardworking homeowners like himself. Now, sadly, thirty years after slaving midnight shifts at Chrysler to purchase him and his then new bride's dream house, Mr. Jessie lived across the street from a virtual war zone. Much like the battles overseas that heartbreakingly took his only son's life, the very same war that left his wife bitter against all people of Middle Eastern descent.

The repeated sounds of random gunshots echoed off the barely standing walls of the many vacant buildings. Kids had no respect for their elders, desperate addicts would rob you blind in broad daylight, and lastly, dope dealers behaved like they were doing the economically stressed Detroit some huge favor by employing a few street runners. Uncut grass, debris-filled lots, discarded broken beer bottles, and glaring lights of scarcely seen ambulances were the homeowner's world.

Exhausted by the state of his reality, Mr. Jessie decided to become somewhat of a one-man army. Taking matters in his own hands, he meant business. He felt it was the only way he and his wife could beat the escalating problem. Patrolling the neighborhood after dark, keeping a detailed activity log for the police, and even joining forces with one of the local ministers, Mr. Jessie was hell-bent on making a change in his lost community.

Well, would you look at that, he continued to move the broom as he watched the day begin. *That same woman that comes over here every morning buying that stuff almost knocked poor Thelma down. It don't make no kind'a sense.* "Hey, there, Thelma," Mr. Jessie angrily spoke out with concern. "Are you okay? Do you need some help?"

Seeing Thelma was being assisted by one of the young men he was watching like a hawk and blamed for most, if not all, of the chaos that happened on the block, he frowned. Mr. Jessie didn't try to ask his sometimes hard-of-hearing neighbor once more after she didn't respond. Instead, he went on with the charade of him cleaning his front porch in hopes to gain some more information. Then, as Mr. Jessie would do every late afternoon, give the information to Reverend Richards, the preacher, who assured him he was working hand in hand with Detroit's newly formed Narcotics Task Force to bring a quick halt to inner-city open-air drug transactions. Mr. Jessie believed in the hope that in between the police, the good reverend, and himself, there could, and would, soon be change. As he stood there, his mind drifted back to the day when he and his new bride first moved into the practically Caucasian-inhabited neighborhood.

The moving truck pulled up in front of the one-story dwelling. Backing up in the driveway, the young man full of life and hope looked over his shoulder. After making sure he wasn't close to hitting one of the brick pillars, he proceeded to park. Killing the engine, he swung the driver's door open and jumped out. A huge grin graced his face as he waved at his wife. She had been following closely behind with a carload of their belongings they hadn't trusted to be in the truck.

"This is it, baby, home sweet home." He was ecstatic that he was able to purchase this fabulous home on his blue-collar factory salary. Standing on his feet night after night was hard work, but now, he was finally able to see the fruits of his labor pay off.

"Oh my God, I know," Mrs. Jessie answered, caught in her emotions. Taking her man's left hand, she held it tight, locking fingers. Swinging their arms back and forth, the pair was content. This was a day they would never forget. Mr. and Mrs. Jessie felt like they had finally "made it." Residing on this block was indeed a dream come true. Although the neighborhood was multicultural, all the residents appeared to get along, loving and respecting their community. Now, the newlyweds could concentrate on having a family and making their lives complete.

***

The annoying sound of his phone jerked the long-time resident of the block back from the days of the past and into harsh reality. His once beloved, admired, and cherished homestead had turned to hell on earth. Ignoring his telephone, Mr. Jessie protectively waited for Thelma to safely make it down the street without any more incidents. Being Block Club president was a job he took seriously. Even when the two main dope-slinging thugs waltzed past his house, acting like they didn't have a care in the world, Mr. Jessie refused to back down, looking each in their eye. His own personal war on illegal substances and the crime that accompanies it was in his front yard.

There's no way in hell I'ma let these hooligans win this fight. No way in hell. This is my neighborhood. Vengefully, he shook his head as one youngster spit a glob of saliva directly on his property as if to say "Fuck you, old man! We do what we wanna do when we wanna do it!" Mr. Jessie, strong willed in spirit, held the broom-stick tightly as if he was some sort of a warrior ready to do battle. *I'ma get y'all one day. Ya think y'all so smart, but one day, the tables are gonna turn—they always do. And when that day comes, I'm gonna be standing in judgment. Then let's see who has the last laugh.*

Chapter Three

Clay

"What's wrong with you—you crazy psycho," he called out to the same female, day after day, that acted entitled, like her shit didn't stink. "The next time you do that foul garbage, your ass ain't getting served! You hear me?"

The rude preppy-dressed customer appeared not to pay her supplier any real attention, slamming her car door shut. Then, as usual, she pulled halfway down the block to get high.

"I'm sorry for cursing, excuse me," Clay addressed the old woman while picking up her cane. "But these heads don't let nothing interfere with them getting 'theirs.'"

Noticing the disapproving expression on her face, Clay excused himself, returning to the stoop as the elderly woman regained her balance, slowly making her way wherever she was headed. No more words needed to be exchanged. It was not as if the two of them had anything in common. Thelma Gale was a nice old lady, but to Clay and his crew, she was just another casualty of the game. Without as much as a single word to even acknowledge Clay was alive, she took a minute a few houses down to, once again, catch her breath. Part of her wanted to sit down and really get herself together but knew from often peeking out her front window, a stray bullet or some other hood antic was liable to bring her harm. No time to be a crime statistic, Thelma soon disappeared off the block and out of Clay's sight

"Man, why do you even try to be nice to these fake motherfuckers around here?" Whip mean mugged the few residents outside trying to maintain some normalcy to their lives as drugs took over their community. "All they asses some snitches. They don't care if we dead or alive," he huffed, taking a twenty-dollar bag of purple out of his pocket. "Like him over there," he arrogantly gestured to a man sweeping his front porch. "I know his faggot ass called the police last week! Shit, wasn't no cops even coming on the block heavy until TimTim and Yuk beat that dopefiend down on his walkway and all them bodies started popping up!"

Clay surveyed the block as his boy complained about the police's occasional, unwanted visits. "Damn, Dorie," he laughed, watching a group of children wait for the school bus. "This guy Whip out here acting like this thang we doing is legal. Like we got a license to slang. We in the game—they ain't. We got a job to do selling this shit and not get caught, and they got a job to do calling the punk-ass police. That's the rules of the game we playing. They just doing what they supposed to do. And they shouldn't care if we live or die."

Whip ripped opened the bag of weed, taking a long whiff of the potent smell. "I know what you saying, but fools like his snitching ass over there, judging people for trying to survive, be killing me."

Clay could once again tell that Whip was caught up in his feelings. Oftentimes when Whip got like that, Clay would give him a minute to come back down to planet Earth. That's what made Clay a good leader. He knew how to make each member on his team feel like they were the captain.

"Yo, Dorie, why don't you go around the corner and check on the other spot real quick? Make sure them li'l dudes stay on they toes." Clay stood to his feet, picking a tiny piece of lint off his white T-shirt. "Me and Whip gonna run up to the store so he can grab an orange juice or something to cool his hotheaded ass off!"

Dorie laughed, leaving Clay and Whip heading in one direction while he headed in the other. When Clay passed the man on his porch sweeping, he nodded his head, knowing the man meant nothing to him. No one could stop his grind was his overall mentality. Whip, on the other hand, made sure to spit on the man's sidewalk as they locked eyes.

"Dawg, leave that old dude the fuck alone," Clay demanded, already fed up with Whip's early-morning bad attitude. "He ain't stopping our shine. He can't." Clay threw his arms up victoriously. "Look around. Ain't nobody out here rolling with him."

Whip did as he was told, leaving the silly madness alone before Clay got heated. "You right, you right."

"I know I am."

Minutes later, they bent the corner, disappearing into the Arab-owned store, not noticing Reverend Richards, who was greeting a few "unfortunate souls," watching them out of the corner of his eye.

Abdul Silah

Leaving the four-family dwelling he called home, fifteen-year-old Abdul Silah, and his little sister did as they always did every morning on their way to school. It was somewhat a ritual to the young man. No sooner than his feet touched the front sidewalk of his house, Abdul wanted to turn around and climb back into his bed. Most kids felt that way about school, so that was considered normal. Unfortunately, it was the other circumstances he was dealing with that made his situation worse.

Prior to the ill-fated 9/11 attack on America, things were bad enough for the awkward, pimpled-faced teenager. Now, after the Twin Towers had come suddenly crumbling down into ruins—it was almost unbearable. He and his family being Muslim meant constantly being ridiculed, disrespected, and threatened. Their chosen faith was proving to be no more than a sharp thorn in young Abdul's side. One he couldn't seem to avoid. If life in the neighborhood wasn't bad enough, he and his sister, by his father's strictly enforced demands, dressed in traditional Muslim garb resulting in not a moment's peace from judgment.

"Dad, please."

"Son, what part of no don't you understand? I know wearing these things make you as well as your little sister feel as if you don't fit in at times—but so be it."

"I know but—"

"But nothing," the elder stared his seed in the eye letting him know he meant business with the teenager. "Life is what it is. And at times, it's not meant to be easy. Allah puts us through many things to test our devotion to him, our loyalty. Following Islam is not just a passing fad to us; this is our way of living. My father followed the rules that were revealed to Prophet Muhammad, peace be upon him. And God willing, I will do my duty as a Muslim and make sure my children follow those rules as well. Now, if you chose to believe in any other religion, or none at all after you come of age, then, it is, of course, your choice."

"I understand, Dad. It's just whenever we go outside somewhere, even school, the mall, or the park, people stare. They tease us and act like we got bombs stashed in our back pockets."

"Look, son, sometimes going against the grain takes strength. And if you don't have that type of strength to

withstand a few people mocking you for submitting to
the will of Allah, then you must not be of my bloodline.
Now, go get your stuff for school together while your
little sister is getting her hair combed. I don't want you
two to be late again to first hour. I'm tired of getting calls
from the office about that. You both definitely leave this
house in enough time."

Knowing he had no win in the one-sided conversation, Abdul did as he was told. Walking by his mother and
younger sibling, he knew it wise to keep his anger and sar-
casm to himself. *I don't know why she's combing her hair
anyhow. She just gonna cover it up with her hijab.*

Ten minutes later, they were out the door taking in
the ghetto sights and sounds. *Dang, why me? I wish
we were just like everybody else around here. It's not
fair.* Science book in hand, Abdul navigated their way
through the busy block. Met by disapproving stares for
the way they were clothed, along with insults from regular hardworking folk and bums alike, had become
a regular occurrence. Some days were better than others, but this was not one of those days. People seemed
to be out tenfold heading toward the church. Abdul and
his sister were in search of a temporary reprieve from
the mockery and ducked into the corner store for refuge. Having to keep a constant look over his shoulder,
he made sure no one was behind them. Hate crimes
against Muslims was at an all-time high, and he didn't
want them to fall victim. Not paying attention to what
was in front of him as he pushed the door open, the teen
stumbled.

"Oh, I'm so sorry. Excuse me, my mistake," Abdul
quickly said to one of the dope dealers he'd recognized
from the block as their shoulders bumped. "I do apologize. I wasn't paying attention."

"Not a problem, young brother; you good," the guy
causally replied as he continued talking to his partner.

Exhaling, Abdul was glad that the guy accepted his apology. He knew from firsthand experience that something as minor as bumping into someone or stepping on a person's shoe could go left really quickly in Detroit, Muslim or not. Heading back to the cooler, he walked by three different glass doors before seeing what he wanted. Going over in his head some of the cruel things a passenger in a car driving by had just yelled, Abdul shook his head as removed a small plastic container of papaya juice. *I'm so tired of people around here not understanding that me and my family are not terrorists. We don't get up every morning trying to figure out how to do harm to America. I mean, dang, could halfway see if we were Middle Eastern; but we black just like them. Not even African black but nigga black.*

Before the troubled teen could pick out a juice for his sister, loud voices from the front of the store immediately snatched his attention. Momentarily pausing, he took a few deep breaths. Abdul saw a small group of boys he easily recognized had entered through the door. *Not again. Not now. The day just started, and now I gotta deal with these idiots.* Feeling the coldness of the bottle in his left hand and clutching his school textbook in the right, Abdul began to sweat. He looked at his innocent sister whose eyes were now twice the size as his. Each got prepared for what foolishness they knew was sure to follow. Running into them had become a "thing" that Abdul didn't want to become an ongoing habit. Yet, on the regular, the excessively rowdy gang horse playing near the counter seemed to make it their life's ambition to torment Abdul for his faith. He prayed they would not be in the immature state of mind they were normally in, but Abdul would have no such luck today. When the childish group started ridiculing the Middle Eastern store owner for the traditional head scarf wrap he was wearing, the nervous teen knew, without a doubt, he and his sister were next. Standing as still as he possibly could, the teenager did his best to not be seen or heard. Using the potato chip rack as a makeshift shield between him and his sister and his tormentors, Abdul tried to scrunch down.

Watching several customers come in and out the door, he wanted to seize the moment. Wanting desperately to avoid confrontation, Abdul saw an opportunity for them to slip out unnoticed. He didn't want any trouble today—or any day, for that matter. All he wanted was for the two of them to go to school in peace, but the chances of that, especially now, were growing slim to none. Slowly creeping toward the doorway, he and his sister were, unfortunately, spotted by one of the guys and loudly called out.

"What up, doe? Ain't this about nothing this damn morning. If it ain't that dress-wearing, swami-ass Ali Baba Negro and his ninja sidekick. What's up, mop head in a dress?" The main leader of the small mob of boys mocked Abdul and his sister's traditional clothing. "What you doing up so early? You must be getting supplies to blow up the school with a bomb later; maybe at lunchtime? Ain't that what y'all do? Or is you sneaking eating a pork sandwich—one of them good Honey Baked Hams with extra glaze?"

All the teens laughed, including a few ill-mannered customers. Abdul didn't bother to answer his classmate's ridiculous insults with a response. He knew if he did, it would only add fuel to the fire. Still holding the juice in his hand he had yet to pay for, he tried stepping around the hostile group that was now surrounding him and his sister.

"Maybe he didn't hear you," another commented blocking Abdul's path while yanking at his sister's hijab, causing her neck to snap backward. "He might need

Allah to help him answer the motherfucking question. Or maybe this little ninja can hear better if we uncover her ears."

"Hey, leave us alone. Don't touch my sister like that. We didn't do anything to you guys." Abdul was terrified of yet another beat down but opted to at least stand his ground for his sister's sake. "I don't want any problems with you all. Please just let us leave." Not knowing what to say or do next, he stood in deep thought. Caught in the moment, he blamed his father for making him and his sister be different, not the out of control teens.

"Hey, you troublemakers, you leave my store right now," the shopkeeper ordered, waving the cordless phone from behind the bulletproof glass. "I'm not playing. I'll call the police on you. Leave now. I'm tired of the same thing every day. Now go and leave them alone."

The leader of the pack didn't care about the threat of the police who never showed up on time anyway. Not used to giving two rotten shits about authority, he spit on the floor of the store, daring the man to place the call. "You funny as hell, immigrant-ass motherfucker. I tell your sand-nigga-ass what; call them and see do I care. Matter of fact—call 'em now, and I bet I'll burn this store to the ground before they show up." Turning his attention back to his intended victims, he wasn't done with them yet. Raising his hand, he slapped the bottle of juice out of Abdul's hand, causing it to shatter on the already dirty floor. Closing his fist tightly, the out of control teenager drew back. Without further warning, he sucker punched the Muslim youth dead in his jaw. Arms flinging, he fell back into a display of can goods. Abdul, obviously dazed, was a soldier and shook the unprovoked hit off. Scrambling to his feet, he grabbed his sobbing sister in hopes of shielding her from any more of the group's attacks that had now shifted from verbal to physical.

Fortunately for Abdul and his sister, there was a reprieve. Before any other blows could be delivered, one of the dealers from the block stepped in.

"Yo, hold up. What the fuck is wrong with y'all li'l kids these days?" he shoved the one who had all the mouth. Immediately after, he then cuffed up the apparent wannabe leader. "He ain't did nothing to y'all trying-to-be-tough idiots. I'm tired of y'all little assholes making it hot around here just the fuck because. Y'all need to fall the fuck all the way back."

"So damn what!" the boy quickly fired back with his chest stuck out. Also raised by the streets, he remained defiant, trying to save face in front of his crew. "He always be walking around here thinking he better than everybody, wearing that gay sissified dress. And look at that little terrorist in training trying to hide that nappy-ass hair of hers. They ain't fooling no-damn-body."

"So what, little nigga? Damn! Is him or this little girl hurting you? Huh? Well—is they? And watch your mouth when you talking to me. I ain't one of these pint-size lames you run with. I'll beat all y'all asses half to death like it ain't shit," Clay angrily proclaimed, pushing the now-silent bully and his cohorts toward the door. "It's too early in the a.m. for this bull. I don't know if y'all done popped some pills or smoked some Kush, but whatever the fuck it is, I'm the one to get y'all little ill-bred youngsters all the way together!"

"Damn, OG, it's like that?" one tried arguing back like he was an even match for Clay.

"Yeah, bitch-made nigga, it's just the fuck like that!"

"But—" he still tried going toe-to-toe.

"Look . . ." Clay had just about enough of the childish word games. He felt his temperature rise. His hand was asking to slap the fuck outta a nigga. Clay knew if he didn't get out of this zone, the worst-case scenario would happen. He grunted and decided to put a final end to it. "Y'all best bet is to just get the fuck on and take y'all badasses to school before I really get pissed and beat the breakfast cereal outta one of y'all. You feel me? You better ask around if you don't know. Y'all must be new to this area, but I'll fuck around and evict you and your ole girl after I have her suck my dick."

"Yeah but—"

"Yeah, my ass. I'm done with this."

"Dawg, you don't understand with your fake light-skin ass. You ain't even black enough to be talking shit to us, calling us all niggas. Matter of fact, you look more like that ho-ass camel jockey behind the counter."

"Now look," Clay cautiously warned, not wanting to skull drag a kid but certainly not above it. "Look, I done said it's too early in the morning for this bullshit. And as for who the fuck I look like or don't look like, you got the game fucked up. Now do you li'l bastards really want it with a real nigga like me or not? It's y'all call." He cracked his knuckles ready to put in a little lightweight work. Tucking his gun deep in his waistband he grinned. "'Cause see, I'm still good with mines. These hands do what they do, and I'll beat a kid's ass just for old time sake."

Abdul stood mute, rubbing his sore jaw. Thankful, he looked on as the boisterous group begrudgingly dispersed from the store, but not before helping themselves to a few bags of hot chips and tipping over the metal newspaper rack.

"As-salaam alaikum," Clay spoke having taken his *Shahadah* while locked up a few years back but was not following Islam any further.

"Wa alakum assalam," Abdul happily responded with relief, still holding his jaw.

"Look, you and your sister go tell Kalif I said to let y'all out the back way. Y'all should be good. If not, holler at me. Don't let them assholes stop you and your sister from being who Allah intended on y'all being. Y'all out here doing the right thing; trust me. Stay true to y'all self."

"*Inshallah*," Abdul announced.

"Yeah, *inshallah*," Clay reaffirmed as Whip looked on, not the least bit interested in Islam, Allah, the Quran, or the Bible, for that matter, or anything they stood for. In Whip's greedy, self-indulged eyes, money—the almighty dollar—was the only God he knew, and the only thing he worshiped.

As the two older guys stood guard making sure the trouble-intent teens left from in front of the doorway entrance, the Muslim store owner did as Clay asked. Unlocking the security door and gate, he allowed his religious-linked little brother and sister out the back exit. Peeking around the corner to make sure the coast was indeed clear, Abdul saw the brazen crew go down the block. They were soon turning their vindictive attentions toward a young mother and her small children.

Extremely grateful for the divine intervention of a beat down, he nodded at Clay holding his right fist up against his heart, signifying respect. *Now maybe we can make it to school or at least to the church. I hate being Muslim and being judged for nothing. It's not fair.*

Abdul grabbed his little sister's hand. Wasting no more time, they ran toward Reverend Richards's Outreach Building. Even though Abdul and the preacher had very different faiths and overall beliefs, the seemingly devoted man of the cloth never once turned him or his sister away when they were being chased, mocked, or ridiculed— which was almost daily. The good reverend had even given Abdul a Bible which the teen snuck and read every night before going to sleep instead of the Quran. He knew if his father ever found out, there would be hell to pay, so Abdul kept it hidden.

Trinity Walker

Damn, when this bus coming? I could be at home still in the bed! With a sleeping newborn in the stroller and balancing a crying toddler on her hip, Trinity peered down the busy block. "Stop that noise. You too big for all that. Now be quiet before you wake your brother," she commanded her son.

Extremely late for her appointment at the Child Support Office, Trinity tried calling her worker, hoping to maybe reschedule but kept receiving the voice mail. Frustrated for even being up this time of morning, she finally got her fussy son calmed down. Using the last few dollars she had on her Bridge Card to buy him a bag of chips and a chocolate milk, she prayed the public transportation she relied on would arrive so she could get back and watch reruns of *Bad Girls Club*.

Not having either of her sons' fathers in their life, the barely out-of-her-teens mother lived month to month the best way she could. From time to time, guys she "dated" would bless her with a free trip to Red Lobster or at least some White Castle, depending on what all she was willing to do with them. Some months were better than others. Luckily, when times were real tight, she'd get a nice-size food box from the Church Outreach Building. It wasn't much in the way of what she and her kids desired to eat, but beggars definitely couldn't be choosers. Bottom line, Trinity Walker and her children were catching it. Then suddenly, out of nowhere, her already bad day was seconds from getting worse.

"Hey, big booty," one boy rudely mocked, smacking Trinity across the rear.

"Dang, she got a fatty—one of them Nicki Minaj asses," another spoke on the young mother's backside as if he was a grown man, not a ninth-grader.

"What the hell!" Trinity turned around with her son still on her hip. Furious, she wasted no time cursing the youths out. "Y'all must've lost y'all's damn mind. You best keep ya motherfucking hands the fuck off me."

"Or what!" a third teen joined in. "You gonna make us drink milk from them big headlights of yours?"

As they all laughed, Trinity caught a glimpse of her young neighbor and his small sister creeping by through the rear alleyway. They were headed in the direction of the Outreach Building where the Reverend Richards had just the day prior blessed her with a few bottles of formula for her baby. Trinity wanted nothing more than to shout at Abdul to come hold her kids while she taught these disrespectful idiots a lesson. However, he and his sibling seemed in a rush. "Look, y'all gonna mess around and catch a foot up y'all ass if y'all don't be careful," she promised with conviction. "I ain't one of y'all little damn friends. Y'all gonna get hurt fucking with me."

"Whatever, bitch."

"Bitch? Oh yeah? I got your bitch, little boy." With all the commotion, both of her small children were now wide awake and crying. Without hesitation, she placed the older of the two on the ground near the stroller and instructed him not to move. Trinity then put her cell in her back pocket, kicked off her flip-flops and irately braced up to fight. "Trust, y'all done fucked up now."

Before Trinity could swing, Clay showed up and intervened. No matter how much she tried to flirt with the hood kingpin in the past, he never paid her a second thought. Now, here he was ready to assume the role of her ghetto hood knight in shining armor, only dressed in Tims. "What in the entire fuck is wrong with y'all? Didn't I already tell y'all to take y'all little punk asses the fuck on? Why y'all out here messing with this lady?"

"Damn, old school, you ain't nobody's daddy," the leader mumbled under his breath as his friends, now intimidated, looked on. "And this tramp ain't no damn lady."

"Yo, did you say something, big man?" Clay, growing angrier, stepped to him. Wrapping his hand around the back of the teen's neck, Clay applied pressure. "I ain't hear you. Matter of fact, while you running your mouth—apologize."

"Well," Trinity, full of attitude, reached down trying to console her children. "Where is all that mouth you just had—all of y'all? Talk *that* bullshit now."

"Sorry," the boy swiftly grimaced in pain before being let loose.

Knowing his boss was seconds from exploding all the way, Whip had to step in, making his presence felt. "You wannabe tough li'l playas—bounce before shit to the point of no damn return. Ain't gonna be no more fucking around with y'all."

Sensing they had caused enough havoc for the morning without getting in serious trouble, the group took Whip's advice and ran off toward the school.

"I wanna thank—" Before Trinity could finish her sentence and hopefully get Clay to maybe sponsor a meal or two or three, his cell rang. All about his business, he immediately stepped over to the side to answer it.

Whip, however, was left ready to capitalize on the moment. As if it was second nature, he glanced down at Trinity's wide ass. He and his boys had seen the young mother around the way for some time, but she was just a little bit too ghetto for his taste. She was very unpolished on the norm. However, she seemed to be looking extra cute today, so Whip figured—why not?

"That wasn't nothing, ma," he stuck his chest out, realizing she had her sights focused on Clay. "What's good with you later on? What's the deal?"

"Well, I'm . . . um . . ." stalling until Clay ended his call and possibly showing her some attention was not working out as planned. Sure, Whip was cute, and she knew he had money to spend, but Clay was the man around the hood. He was the big fish. Fucking with him could be her big payday. Any female that ran his pockets would be straight for a long time to come. Just thinking about that drunk and damn near toothless Ida's granddaughter Rhonda, whom she'd enviously seen Clay with the past month or so, was proof enough in the way her once raggedy-weave-wearing ass had come up. *Damn! Ain't this about nothing. Of all the times for DOT to show up.* Trinity couldn't believe her luck. After running late, the bus finally decided to turn the corner, cutting her impromptu game plan short.

"Look, ma, whenever you get back from wherever, come find me on the block, okay?" Whip still kept trying his hand even after helping her put the stroller onto the bus.

Through the fingerprint smeared bus window, Trinity watched Clay and Whip walk back down the block. All day long she would think about Clay coming to her rescue. Forget Whip. Clay was the hog with the big ones. The farther the bus drove, the more Trinity drowned the annoying sounds of her kids out. She continued to stare out the window and daydream what her life could be like if she were childless and Clay's main woman. She knew there would be no way in hell she'd be on the bus. She'd be pushing a new Benz or SUV every season.

Trinity imagined all the shopping sprees Clay would sponsor and the over-the-top trips they would take here, there, and all over the world. Held captive by her fantasy, Trinity was pulled back into her real everyday, humdrum, below-poverty existence. Another passenger on the bus was nudging her arm to alert her that the baby had dropped its bottle. *Damn, I hate this fucked-up life I done made for myself. And I double hate y'alls daddies for being some deadbeat bum-ass niggas,* she regretfully glared at her seeds.

Chapter Four

Clay

Tuesday morning rolled around, and it was back to the same routine as the day before; trying to survive in Detroit the best way a midlevel hustler knew how. Needing to pick up a few much-needed supplies to keep his ever-growing enterprise on the rise and standing tall, Clay yawned, fighting to get out of his king-sized bed which he shared from time to time with a female of his choice. Last night and the few weeks prior—it was Rhonda. Having got down with her from time to time in hotels, motels, and short stays all around Metro Detroit, he finally trusted her semienough to bring her to the Grosse Pointe apartment complex where he laid his head at. No girl in Detroit could really be trusted when it came down to it, but Rhonda knew enough to know if she ever crossed Clay, the consequences wouldn't be worth the crime. It'd be her last day on earth. She, like everyone else, could see by the cold and dark uncertain gaze in Clay's eyes—he took loyalty seriously. It was strange to some, but whenever a person even thought about or considered crossing Clay, he would give them that "evil eye" of his, and they immediately fell back.

Feeling him move around in the bed, the "flavor of the month" started to wake up as well. Rhonda was just average in the looks and in the body department, but it was her street edge that made a dude like Clay first take notice of her. Not scared to ride dirty, guns, dope, pills or talk that gangster-girl slang when she felt like she was getting taken advantage of, it was what it was. Rhonda was what most guys in Clay's position searched a lifetime for: a true, authentic, bottom bitch. Most times, the slicked-mouth diva knew her position and played it, but like most females, she'd step out of line from time to time and had to be brought back down to the reality of dealing with a balla—especially one of Clay's caliber.

"Yo, get up, girl. Wake that ass up." He nudged her shoulder as she resisted taking the sheet off her head. "We gotta roll. You know I don't like keeping my folk waiting."

"Dang, Clay. Why can't I stay here while you handle your business? I can go grab some groceries and hook up some dinner later."

Clay stood to his feet. Standing in the mirror thinking about getting several more tattoos, he laughed at her daily repeated request. "Come on, now, Rhonda. How many times do we have to go through this routine? Is you slow or something? You already know how I stand on that type of bullshit."

"But, Clay," she whined relentlessly in hopes of getting her way.

"But Clay what? Where in the fuck is we really going with this one-sided conversation?" Naked in all his glory, he headed toward the shower, towel in hand. "Now look, I'm about to wash these here nuts, you feel me? And you can either come in there and help a brother out or stay out here and get your clothes on; either way, we both breaking out when I get dressed. The bargaining session is over."

Mad she'd never been able to stay alone at his suburban apartment and nose around at free will, Rhonda got tangled in her overwhelming love for Clay. She'd more than proved she was "down for whatever" when it came to him on more than a few occasions, but Clay was adamant about his rules. "I swear to God this fool think somebody out to get him—with his overly paranoid ass," she arrogantly mumbled. "If I wanted to get him, trust and believe, he'd already be got! He think driving around ten more minutes and bending all them corners late at night gonna have my ass confused where I'm at? He crazy as fuck."

Yearning for nothing more than to get a few more hours of sleep and lie around like she was wifey, Rhonda hesitantly did as she was told. As the cold air conditioner climate hit her chocolate skin causing her to get chill bumps, she looked over at the nightstand. Seeing Clay's cell as well as his wallet, she thought she'd take her chances and see what was really good with the man she was so devoted to that obviously wasn't returning the favor.

Letting her curiosity take over, her eyes darted toward the bathroom door, ensuring the coast was clear. Opening his wallet first, she discovered no big surprises as she snooped; his driver's license, registration, and insurance papers to a few cars that she already knew were in someone else's name and a spare key to the truck. Besides an old photograph of him and a woman who had to be his mother, Rhonda came up empty-handed with any potential dirt or clues to who he really was.

Glancing at the hallway, she remained motionless, making sure Clay wasn't coming back. Taking a deep breath, she reached for his phone. Relieved he didn't have a lock or special code, she exhaled. Wishing she didn't have such long nails, she fumbled with each icon she touched, bringing up a different screen. First, incoming calls, then outgoing—she copied down the numbers and names she didn't recognize, tucking the paper in her purse. "This sneaky wannabe playa got too much going on for my black ass," she remarked in a whisper before tapping the envelope icon revealing his existing text messages and reading them as quickly as possible. Seeing that she wasn't the only female vying for his attention, her heart started to ache.

Placing his cell back where she'd found it, Rhonda fell back onto the pillow wishing she and Clay could be much more than apparent fuck buddies. Daydreaming what their kids would look like, she went so far as to think of names of their twins; one a boy and one a girl. Rhonda was fascinated by Clay's good hair and extra fair skin, so she automatically assumed their joint offspring would be gorgeous. She couldn't help but grin as she thought about her perfect fantasy. However, the only roadblock standing in the way of fulfilling that family dream was only a few yards away, hell-bent on being a single street nigga his entire life.

"Hey, yo, Rhonda! Bring your hot firecracker ass in here and give your manz some of that head game you working with," Clay snatched her out of her emotions.

Rhonda might have felt slighted; yet, she was not going to pass on an opportunity to please her future baby daddy. Hearing the shower water still running, she was soon met by a thick mist of steam when she opened the bathroom door, stepping inside. After joining Clay in a round of early-morning sexual escapades, the sometimes ill matched couple got themselves together. Sixteen or so minutes later, the pair was out the door climbing in Clay's midnight-colored leased Hummer. After bending a few corners in the dismal morning climate, Clay was dropping a tight-lipped Rhonda off at the lower-income area two-family flat she shared with her mother, two older sisters, a nephew, four cousins, as well as her drunk drug-addicted grandmother Ida.

Seeing the screen door damn near falling off the hinges and dirty diapers thrown out on her front porch, Rhonda rolled her eyes at her existing living conditions. Up until the moment she started hanging with Clay and was exposed to a carefree lifestyle, she didn't know any better. The downtrodden hood rat had accepted her circumstances as normal. However, one taste of the so-called good life, the eager-to-please girl resented the world for the hand she was dealt at birth. Angry, not being able to just chill, relax, and enjoy the tranquility at Clay's apartment, Rhonda tried her best to play it off. She knew just as easily as he'd noticed her around the way, he could do the same to the next female that was always waiting in the wings as her replacement.

"Baby, will I see you later?" Uncertainty filled her voice after shutting the truck's door. Clay was busy calling Whip while ignoring Rhonda's questions that wouldn't stop coming. "Well, Clay, will I? What time you gonna pick me up tonight, huh?" she presumably asked, refusing to take no for an answer or be placed on the back burner. "I can be ready whatever time you say."

Shrugging his shoulders at her barrage of questions, Clay pulled off from the curb, not having time to deal with Rhonda's mixed Kleenex tissue sentiments. The street drug pharmacist had less than thirty minutes to get on the block, hook up, and set up the new package. Although he had a small amount of product left from the night before, it definitely was not enough to satisfy his loyal clientele. With a one-track mind, nothing or no one would stop Clay making money, especially a wet bottom female.

"Yeah, Whip, I just dropped her worrisome ass off." He looked in his rearview mirror referring to Rhonda. "She's beginning to be a bug. Ain't no girl worth all that mouth, you know what I'm saying? This bird never stops with the third-degree. Females need to know when to fall back!"

"Man, I told you before you started hitting her, she and her family was cut like that; three generations of begging Negroes—from the grandmother on down. Straight headache hoes!"

"Yeah, well, that part-time jumpoff about to run its course, but in the meantime, holler at Dorie and tell him I'll be there in about fifteen or twenty." Clay mashed the gas pedal, checking his watch. "I need to make a few stops first; then I'm official."

As he turned the gas-guzzling Hummer into the parking lot of the West Side CVS he frequently visited, Clay noticed it was growing increasingly cloudy. *Aww, damn, it's about to be messed up.* He figured it was looking like rain which always slowed down business. *Guess I gotta run a special on that work.*

After recounting the rubber banded money in his pockets, Clay got pissed knowing good and damn well it was $350 short of what it was supposed to be. He'd added his cash up the night before. Wrapping a different color band around each knot according to what he had to purchase, Clay knew Rhonda had to have hit him up. More than likely while he was posted in the shower. *Fuck it, that tagalong really done tore her ass this time. I hate a thief! A lying motherfucker is one thing, but a thief is another. Well, she done—on to the next one.*

Before getting out of the truck, Clay erased Rhonda's contact information from his cell phone altogether, including any text messages. Since he never answered any strange, unknown random numbers—by her own conniving hand, Rhonda was history. Gangster girl, ride-or-die tendencies or not—from this point on, that's all Rhonda was—past tense.

Chapter Five

Unlikely Allies

Having waited for the constantly late DOT bus to arrive, Thelma Gale's heart was heavy. She would have to try to figure out what excuse she was going to give the cashier at the pharmacy if the copay amount exceeded the funds in her small change purse. With shaky hands, one clutching the handle of her cane, Thelma stepped off the bus. Making her way inside the virtually empty CVS, she sighed.

"Well, hello, there, Mrs. Gale. Nice to see you," the pharmacist trainee greeted the elderly woman who was a regular. "How are you this fine morning?"

"Hello, dear. I'm doing well. Thanks so much for asking." Thelma smiled, happy that someone was taking the time to share a kind word with an old woman.

"Mrs. Gale," the white jacket-clad head pharmacist rudely interrupted while watching the store's entrance, "your doctor called in your prescriptions late yesterday. There are a grand total of three different ones this time."

"Three did you say?"

"Yes, three prescriptions in total. One is covered by your insurance, but the others—the copay—cost almost twenty dollars for them both." He sent his trainee to get the stapled closed bags. "So should I have them rung up for you or what?"

"Twenty dollars you say?" Thelma was at a loss, knowing she had only a ten-dollar bill and two crumbled up singles to her name. "Well, let me see what I'm going to do."

Seeing the person he was waiting for come through the double glass doors, the pharmacist's entire demeanor got disrespectful in tone. The Indian beige-skinned pharmacist grew increasingly short in patience, shooing the grandmother to the side to figure out her own financial hardships. "Hello, Clay. What's happening?"

"Nothing much guy, just trying to survive. What you got for me?" Inconspicuous as possible, Clay leaned over the counter, sliding the man a small folded knot of money.

Looking down the semiempty aisles, then giving a subtle glance up at the security cameras, the pharmacist told Clay to give him a minute or two to get rid of possible prying eyes. Getting handed three separate bags from his trainee, he then raised his voice at the elderly, financially stressed woman. "Well, what's it going be, Mrs. Gale? What are you going to do?"

"I'm still trying to see which one I need the most."

"You obviously need them all. That's why the doctor prescribed them."

When Thelma looked up to respond to his callous comment, she recognized Clay as the same young man on her block that had helped her the day prior from almost being trampled by a girl buying her morning blast. "Umm, I know that, young man, it's just that—"

"Just what is it this time, Mrs. Gale?" he feverishly replied as if he was fed up with the trivial back-and-forth conversation. "It's always something with you!"

Clay couldn't believe his ears and the way this fool was addressing the old lady—an old *black* lady, no less. Forgetting about the illegal business at hand, the otherwise coldhearted cocaine hustler started to feel some sort of way. "Damn, man, why in the hell you talking to her like that? Have you lost your damn mind or something?" His chest grew swollen with anger and scorn.

"Excuse me? What?" The pharmacist was thrown off by Clay's reaction and tried explaining. "You don't understand. Every few weeks, it's the same routine with the lady, Mrs. Gale. If you don't have the money, then why even bother to show up here? It's common sense."

"You right! I don't understand—I over damn stand!" Seeing the look of shame on the old woman's face, Clay grew infuriated, coming to her rescue. "Look, Ankit," he called him by his first name. "I don't know how y'all treat old people where the fuck you come from, but that low-key fly disrespect ain't bumping around here!" Even though Clay spoke to Ida and every other old drug addict like they were no more than a piece of hot dog shit on a stick, he recognized this old woman was a civilian to the street game.

"But, Clay, I'm not running a charity mission. I can't give medicine away for free."

"Who in the fuck said that crazy-sounding garbage? Not me," Clay sneered at the trainee who stood back silent. "But you damn straight ain't gotta talk all reckless! Sorry for cursing," he directed his last comment to Mrs. Gale. "But this fool ain't gonna be all up in a black neighborhood blowing that garbage out of his mouth."

Struggling to stand on her weak knees, the grandmother mouthed the words "thank you" before solemnly heading toward the exit door leaving the prescriptions, even the one that was covered by her insurance.

"Man, you's a motherfucker! How much is the medicine?"

"Twenty dollars."

"Twenty damn dollars." His voiced echoed throughout the store, causing other customers, including the renta-cop security guard, to take notice. "That's all, and you talking to an old woman like that? Dude, someday a nigga gonna fuck you up in this motherfucker. Shit, if that was my granny, you'd been dead. Now here," Clay peeled off a twenty, tossing it onto the counter. "Now hurry the fuck up and give me that medicine and my package so I can catch her. And, Ankit, I swear for God, if I come back in this store and catch you mouthing off at anybody's mama or old-ass grandma like that again—it's gonna be a no fly zone around this son of a bitch for you!"

Why, Lord, why? As a humiliated, defeated Thelma stood at the bus stop, she didn't bother to look up as Clay eased his truck up to the curb, bringing it to a stop.

Snatching up the three bags of prescription pills off his passenger seat, he jumped down from the truck. "Excuse me, ma'am. I was just inside CVS with you."

"Oh yes," she held her cane tightly, trying to have some pride about herself. "I pray my problems didn't get you in any trouble, young man. I wouldn't want that."

"No, ma'am. I'm fine," Clay cleared his throat. "I didn't mean to disrespect you with the words I was using in there but—"

"No, it's fine, son. I appreciate what you said, but that man is right. I didn't have the money." Her voice lowered, sounding conquered. "I didn't mean to waste his time."

"All of that bullshit, I mean foolish mess he was talking doesn't matter. I took care of it for you." Handing the bags to Mrs. Gale, Clay felt a strange sense of satisfaction coming over him being able to help.

"Oh my goodness," she said, overjoyed. She smiled not believing what was happening and the blessing she was receiving. "Young man, you didn't have to do this. I would have managed somehow—God willing."

Clay returned her smile. "You're much too pretty to have to 'manage' anything. Here, miss, I wanna give you something else too."

"Me?" Thelma blushed at the young man she always knew to be nothing more than a troublemaker running havoc on her block. "You've done more than enough. I already don't know how I can repay you. God is gonna bless you."

"Knowing my luck, probably not—but just take this, please." Usually having zero tolerance with people in general, Clay handed her two $100 bills like it was nothing. "I know you don't respect where it came from, but that doesn't matter to me. You need it, and I have it to spare—so take it. That should be enough to get your prescriptions for a while and at least take a cab home." He looked at the clouded sky. "It looks like rain."

"But, son—" With aged, wrinkled fingers, she tried to argue, balancing herself on her cane.

"Listen, I would take you on the block myself—right to your front door, but what would your good neighbors say?" he sarcastically chuckled, hailing a cab. "Take care, Mrs. Gale." Clay then surprised the old woman again, remembering her name before walking back to the driver's side of the truck, then speeding off.

Clay hit the block, and like always, it was on and popping. He'd been a little late, but that didn't stop the flow of the business taking place. With his right and left hands, Dorie and Whip on point, Clay knew the early-morning rush of customers would be good. As he drove up two houses down from the spot and parked, he noticed an old-school once-playa-now-turned-wide-eyed rock smoker standing close to Whip. Clay knew whenever Hustle-Man showed up, a horse and pony show was sure to follow.

Damn, it's too early for this clown. I already know he gonna be on some old, wild-style dumb shit. Hesitating to even step foot outside his truck, Clay could tell by the expression on Whip's face if he didn't intervene quick, fast, and in a hurry, old Hustle-Man was on his way to getting his ass handed to him on a silver platter. "Okay, motherfucker," Clay was ready for the scheming to start, "what kinda scam you trying to run this morning? Who you done fucked over?"

"It ain't no kinda scam, ya hear what I'm saying?" Hustle-Man attempted to explain while acting like someone was in hot pursuit. "It's like this here. My people—"

"What, nigga?" Whip laughed, watching him go through his twice a week, three times a day routine of acting like he was still making thangs happen in the hood. "So now you gots people? Who in the fuck is your people—like you's a boss?"

"Slow down, Whip." Clay had to laugh as well. "Maybe this damn near expired fool is reviving the new world order of dope users; some type of union and fraternity mess."

Adjusting his filthy jeans and oil-soiled T-shirt, Hustle-Man ignored the young boys' comments and insults. "Listen here, Clay. Last night a friend of a friend of a friend's cousin got caught slipping."

"Slipping?" Clay quizzed, trying to finally see what the old head was talking about. "What in the hell you mean slipping? Slipping on what?"

Hustle-Man, paranoid, looked around once more. "Well, what I'm 'bout to turn you on to gonna cost you."

"Life cost, nigga, so just come the fuck on and spit it out before I bounce," Clay ordered as Whip folded his arms. "I ain't got no time for fun and games, Hustle-Man. Now, what's the deal?"

"Okay, okay. It's like this." He knew his time was up for stalling. "This dude drive a truck for Walmart—one of those big ones. He was supposed to be in Toledo this morning—at a warehouse."

"And?" Whip tried speeding the story along, seeing Dorie coming back with their breakfast orders. "We about to break bread, fool, so *and what?*"

"And he was with me and my girl last night getting high."

"So what, old head? Y'all was getting high. What's so new about that bullshit?"

"This the part that's new and is gonna cost you big time. But if you want me to go over across on Twelfth Street with the deal, I can." No sooner than he called himself threatening them, he knew he'd gone too far.

Clay and Whip both had enough of the cat-and-mouse game. As they each turned away, leaving Hustle-Man standing there, he saw his golden opportunity to come up on some product, probably more than an eight ball, growing weaker by the second.

"Wait, wait—hold up. Well, he fucked around and got some raw and a half ounce on credit from one of the Twelfth boys. And you know how them boys do. Twenty-four hours and you pay or get beat down or even killed."

Clay stopped dead in his tracks. Turning around, he looked Hustle-Man in his face. "Look, Negro, I know good and damn well you ain't practically hold me and my manz hostage, making our food get cold, on no dummy mission."

"Naw, naw, it ain't like that," he urged them to listen. "The man gave me and my girl the key to his rig and the whole trailer."

At that moment, Clay and Whip realized what Hustle-Man was attempting to say. Hearing that the small-size trailer was parked behind an old, abandoned apartment building, stashed in the deep unkempt trees, grass, and bushes that were common sights in Detroit, made Clay more than interested. The normally nickel-and-dime con man made the streetwise opportunist an offer he couldn't refuse. If they somehow busted the lock open on the Walmart secured trailer and it was filled, with no matter what, Clay would pay him. They agreed $500 would be a fair price, but they would have to act quickly before Walmart discovered the driver hadn't showed up in Toledo and reported the vehicle, along with their stock, missing.

Detroit's Police Department wasn't big on trying to locate stolen cars; however, this particular theft would be highly publicized. Every investigative reporter in town would be taking the opportunity to drag down even more the already rotten-labeled name of the city. Besides, as desperate as times were in the Detroit, whoever found an unattended trailer full of goods would clean it out first before, if even, alerting the authorities their damn self.

Grabbing several huge crowbars from the basement of the spot, Clay got three of his runners to steal Chrysler minivans from the nursing home employee parking lot less than a mile away to haul some of the stolen merchandise he was anticipating. Clay warned Hustle-Man that if this was some dry run dummy mission they was on, he would pay the consequences. He would have Whip go ham, splitting his skull clear down to the white meat.

Eighteen minutes later, they were in a small convoy with Hustle-Man leading the way.

Clay wasn't a fool. He was far from interested in possibly getting caught up in his Hummer, no matter how much stolen goods it could carry. Damn running the risk of his truck being seized if caught up, so he rode with Whip, leaving Dorie to hold down the block until they returned.

After bending a few corners, Hustle-Man pointed over toward the left rear side of an old, dilapidated, six-story building that should've been torn down years ago. There, tucked back behind in plain sight, was the prize just as Hustle-Man had promised. The big blue letters spelling out Walmart was clear as day. Wasting no more time than necessary, the street-wise thugs used the crow bars prying the huge silver locks off. Grabbing the metal handles, they yanked open the small-size trailer.

"What in the—hell, yeah!" Clay smiled joined by Hustle-Man, who knew he was about to get paid.

"What the—maybe we need to renegotiate, young blood." His eyes grew wider than the drugs he smoked usually made them.

"Naw, dude, fall the fuck back. A deal is a deal," Clay announced as he, Whip, and the three workers started unloading everything the three vans and the car could carry.

From flat screens to diapers to aspirin and underwear, the vans were soon packed to the ceilings. Several trips in, the surely now-reported stolen trailer and its contents, all property of Walmart, was completely empty. Paying all the workers, a.k.a. van thieves, a few dollars along with some merchandise, Clay had hit a real lick thanks to Hustle-Man. Peeling off twenty-five twenties, Clay paid the promised fee. Hustle-Man, in turn, was happy to hand Whip back five of them for some much-needed product for him and Ava to smoke.

As for paying the huge drug debt from the night before, the truck driver, who was hiding out in a vacant house thinking about what lie he could tell his boss, let alone the pissed dealer, was on his own. There was no honor amongst thieves, let alone baseheads.

Chapter Six

Clay

"Damn, it's been a long-ass day." Clay ate a red velvet cupcake looking out the window, watching an always nosy Mr. Jessie pretend to be picking paper up from his front yard. *Just keep doing you, old man, and stay outta my lane, and we gonna stay good.*

"Yo, Clay, come see if this is straight." Whip struggled, holding the metal TV mount up on the wall as Dorie grabbed the drill. "I know it's only twenty-seven inches, but I still want this mug straight and right where I can see it when I be counting that bread and getting them little niggas straight on they grind."

Finishing off his Dollar Store snack, Clay came in the living room of the spot laughing. "Are y'all two clowns serious—mounting that tiny screen on the wall? Throw that thing on an old milk carton and keep it moving. It's about time we called it a day."

With the house they used every morning to chill in filled with stolen merchandise, Whip was determined to bring one of the televisions to the work spot to have something to watch when things got slow. Clay knew his boy Whip was easily impressed by irrelevant stuff, so he let him do his thing. If throwing Whip a little extra to keep him happy and loyal, so be it.

Seeing the girl from the bus stop coming back from wherever she'd went to, Whip tried to impress her, promising an iPod or at least a MP3 Player whenever they hooked up. Hopefully, by midnight, Whip planned to be banging the young mother's back out the frame.

Dorie wasn't in the mood for dealing with the neighborhood rats or the many problems that they had with them. He gathered his belongings and made his way to the front porch. Yawning, he made the announcement he had a date with a hot shower and his own bed.

When asked was he hanging with Ida's granddaughter tonight, Clay didn't smile one bit, remaining silent, obviously in deep thought.

Making sure everything was everything and the spot was secure, all three, Clay, Whip, and Dorie, parted ways for the night.

The next morning, Clay woke up, alone this time, with a new attitude in his game plan for the day. Strangely for him, he couldn't stop thinking about the old woman on the block who basically needed twenty dollars to survive. That was the same amount he spent on juice and chips in one hour. When he got on the block today, he was going to make sure the grandmotherly woman would be set, at least for a few months. He thought about how her family must not have been about much, but that wasn't gonna stop his mission and what he had in mind.

Turning his cell back on after constant calls from who could only be Rhonda all night long, Clay was met with over seven voice mails and eight texts confirming that she was either crazy as a fuck or yearning for an ass kicking. *Silly trick spend the night a few nights in a row and think they the wife—these birds these days!* Clay got dressed and left, heading for the hood for another day of same ole same.

As he and his team arrived on the block, Clay saw many of the same faces, waiting for that early-morning blast to get their day started. Customers waiting on them signified they still had good strong product and the day would flow smooth. Dorie had done what he said, getting a good night's sleep, and was in the right state of mind to get money—no distractions. Whip, however, on the other hand, had stayed up half the night knocking the value off the ghetto broad from the bus stop. In between listening to her babies cry, smoking weed, drinking shots of Hennessy, and trying to stop her from asking so many questions about his boss Clay—he was wired up, ready to explode.

Preoccupied, still thinking about the old woman from the day before at CVS, Clay glanced up at the window he would sometimes see her looking out of. Peeping across the street, he then saw the same uppity, smoked-out woman pull up in the silver Toyota Corolla to cop. He shook his head and smirked that she always acted as if she was better than the rest of their clientele. When in all due honesty, she was just another crackhead in search of a head blast. After making sure his team was up and pumping, Clay informed both Dorie and Whip that he was going to make a run and would be back in a few.

"Hey, y'all, hit me up if that old lady upstairs leave out," he firmly demanded as a Water Department van suspiciously drove past. The sound of the occupants' voices made all three, including nosy Reverend Richards that was walking up on Mr. Jessie's porch, take notice.

"What old lady?" Whip questioned, looking around confused as he brushed his deep waves, craving a beer. "And who the hell was that in that motherfucker looking all hard this way?"

"Dawg," Clay nodded his head upward at the window with the beige lace curtains while watching the dark blue van disappear off the block, "the one the crazy basehead over there in that Toyota almost knocked down the other day—*that* old lady. Think, Whip!"

"Ohhhh, yeah, okay, her," Whip vaguely remembered the incident despite all the weed he smoked and Lean he drank. "Why you give a damn about her leaving? What, she calling the police like that good-snitching faggot over there?" He pointed to Mr. Jessie, who, for once, was sitting on his front porch with his wife, minding his own business before their ordained visitor arrived. "Want me to bust her over the head with her cane? 'Cause I can—it's nothing!"

"What the fuck you say about doing to her?" Immediately hyped and heated in the moment, Clay loudly cut him off from the mini-interrogation Whip was conducting. "Dawg—just do what the hell I said! Dorie, you need to talk to this hardheaded dude right here. He on some other type of crazy shit I ain't feeling today. That rotten-boxed cat you got from that girl last night got you out of order! You being too extra! Check yourself before I do it for you! And, oh, yeah—give that uppity broad the smallest rock we got and make her rude ass stand in line just like everybody else!"

Dorie just shook his head at Whip and the foul mood he'd put Clay in as he pulled off. "Why you always getting under that guy skin? You know he'll flip out at any time for anything!"

"Yeah, I know, but lately, he really been on edge, like a ticking time bomb!" Whip made notice while pointing for the "better than the next smoker" to get to the end of the line as Clay had instructed. "Something just ain't right in dawg head!"

Chapter Seven

Trinity Walker

Damn, I really played myself last night for this old thang. I could've came up if I would've just kept my legs closed and my mouth shut. Fumbling with the headphones and iPod Whip had given her the night before in what could only be labeled payment for some ass, Trinity was now regretting him hitting the pussy every which way but loose. *Dang, I sucked that crazy drunk fool off twice and even fucking swallowed, and he gives me this shit right here and a few dollars for grocery and diapers! At least I don't have to go to the freaking Outreach Building today for food and deal with that mess! But, damn, I hope he don't tell Clay we got down!*

Each step the young slum-minded mother took while pushing both children stuffed in a stroller made for one, was full of denial. After Clay coming to her rescue at the bus stop, she believed, if only in her naive mind, she now still had a chance with him even though his worker had been there, done that. The fact that she'd given Whip her cell number and not Clay that morning mattered none. In Trinity's delusional fairy-tale way of thinking, Clay would have checked Whip for trying to push up on her in the first place and demand he give him the number. *If his phone wouldn't'a rung at that moment, he would've stepped to me instead of ole boy. I know he would've.*

Her small mind raced with scattered mixed thoughts and emotions turning the iPod power on. Pausing to put both earphones in to drown out the sound of her smallest child crying, Trinity placed the volume as high as it could go, blasting the factory sample predownloaded music. *I wanna walk down there and see if Clay is posted yet, but Whip might be with him.* Continuing to push the dirty secondhand stroller through the rough crime-infested neighborhood, the otherwise street-educated female navigated her way toward the grocery store, passing a few late-for-school stragglers.

"Hello, Miss Trinity," the always polite young man spoke while cautiously glancing over his shoulder, holding his sibling's hand. Both children's faces appeared worried, but with them, that was normal.

Waving her hand up at the young Muslim teen and his little sister she would see every morning on their way to school, Trinity kept her pace up, wanting to get to the store and back before her shows came on.

Caught in her thoughts about what her life could be with Clay, especially if Whip kept his mouth shut, Trinity didn't notice a dark-colored Ford cargo van with painted windows bend the corner and try to lure Abdul and his sister inside, offering them a ride to school. As the music blasting out of the earphones deadened the van's muffler, along with the baby's constant cries, she went across the shortcut everyone in the hood used. Eleven abandoned houses in a row with overgrown grass, thick bushes along with littered-filled vacant lots shielded her view from most people who didn't know the area or dared not take that route. Trinity, however, felt the rules didn't apply to her. That attitude is probably what caused her to bounce from foster home to foster home growing up.

Foolishly cutting across the alleyway, Trinity was stopped by the slow-cruising vehicle turning directly in her path. "Hey, what in the fuck? Don't you see . . ." Before the words of anger could escape her mouth, the van came to a complete stop. Surprisingly, two men jumped out of the side of the vehicle's sliding doors as the driver kept the loud van idling—serving as a lookout.

"Shut the fuck up. Ain't nobody playing around with your slutty ass."

Rushing up on her, the heavier of the two snatched Trinity by the waist with one hand, covering her mouth with the other, causing her to drop the iPod on the ground, shattering the screen. "Don't say nothing. I mean it—not nothing!"

"Yeah, girl, don't say shit. Just come give us some of that tight cat you got stuffed up in them little shorts!" With the right earphone plug still dangling, she now noticed they were Water Department employees by their badges and clothing. The next thing she knew, one of them had snatched both her kicking feet from the pavement.

Completely unable to break free, the young mother struggled to move. Knowing what was sure to come next, she squirmed, trying her best to fight them off. As she bit down on the side of the first man's filthy hand, he raised his other, socking her in the side of her temple, almost knocking her unconscious. From then on, everything seemed to go in slow motion. Roughly tossing her down onto a pile of old shingles that undoubtedly had blown off a roof, her head turned to the side as her eyes filled with tears. Breast now exposed to the morning air, Trinity, numb, listened to her children's cries of wanting their mother to keep pushing them. Somehow, the pair of blue uniformed rapists managed to practically rip her denim jean shorts almost completely off.

Fighting to see at least the dark-colored wheels of the baby stroller that was only feet away, Trinity shook with fear as the now three men argued over who was gonna get the pussy first. Inhaling the sewer musty smell of one kneeling over her with his manhood inches away from her mouth promising her and her kids death if she bit him, the normally feisty female had given up all hope of not becoming a statistic and decided to comply. Seconds after one man had entered her vagina and the other her mouth, the third man suddenly yelled out, being surprised by a gun being pointed in his face.

"Both of y'all dirty motherfuckers get the fuck up," Clay's voice shouted with intense anger. "Hurry the fuck up before I shoot y'all motherfucking dicks off! What in the fuck is wrong with y'all old, perverted fools—raping a woman with all this free pussy around here they giving away?" He now had all three men lined up along the rear of a garage as he helped a still-dazed, very-much ashamed and hysterical Trinity to her feet. "I outta blast all three of you fucked-up-in-the-head slimeball niggas. I knew some foul business was up when I seen this piece of junkyard-ready-Water-Department-shit y'all driving pulled up back here."

Trinity tried to cover herself the best she could. Disoriented, she wobbled past the city-owned van over toward the stroller. Taking a light receiving blanket out of the bottom, she tried to at least wrap it around her still exposed vagina. Taking both crying kids out, she raised them up, hugging each one, not thinking she'd ever have another chance to do so.

"Wait, young dawg, wait," the heavier guy with a gold tooth bargained for their lives. "She wanted to do it. She told us to come back here, and she'd hit us off for a little bit of change. That's how it went down. I swear—she wanted it."

"He lying, Clay; his ugly fat ass lying," Trinity argued back, defending her character, putting both children back down. Now coming to her senses, getting pissed, she shouted across the alley, "I was just going to the store with my kids, and they jumped out of nowhere. I was minding my own goddamn business." Enraged, she started to cry even more, ready to fight buck naked, it need be. "Y'all old bastards overpowered me. That one grabbed me from the back, and that motherfucker held my feet." Trinity searched finding a huge sharp piece of metal near the very pile of shingles she was just on and lunged at them wanting revenge. "I'ma fuck y'all up! I'ma kill all y'all!"

Clay, already salty, wasn't in the mood for the back-and-forth exchange. On a ten plus, he was far from a fool and hated being played for one. "Look, punk ass! Do it look like I'm slow or something like that? Even Stevie Wonder can see what the fuck y'all was doing. I should let ole girl fuck y'all asses up. I seen y'all earlier cruising the block like y'all was the police or some shit, and y'all out here on the clock," Clay's trigger finger grew extremely jumpy. "How many other females y'all done raped? How many little kids on they way to school y'all done stalked and molested? And how many old people y'all done fucked around and robbed? Damn predators, and y'all work for the Water Department! I'ma give y'all what you need!"

"It's not like that," the other one tried to proclaim while urinating on himself, wanting nothing more than to get back in the van unharmed, drive away, and turn off some poor family's water, he begged. "Just let us go. We sorry, man. Just let us go or call the police." Knowing with the latter of the two, they would at least have a chance to fight the case.

"Police? Call the damn police? Around here, I *am* the fucking police around these parts! *I'm* the mayor of this zip code. Y'all should've done y'all homework before y'all came to this hood with that nonsense—raping a female in front of her kids. But on some for real for real, y'all definitely gonna learn today." Clay had a menacing grin on his face, letting the three uniformed workers along with Trinity know that wasn't gonna happen. Wasn't nobody getting "just let go" and wasn't no police that wasn't gonna show up nohow, getting called; at least not without some blood being shed for retribution for them having the nerve to come into his neighborhood trying to violate.

"Come on now, homeboy, please!" The driver negotiated for his own life, throwing his partners in crime underneath the bus. "I didn't even touch her! Ask her—I didn't! I didn't even want to do it!"

"All y'all nasty old motherfuckers got exactly five seconds to decide whose dick she gonna cut off with the metal shit she holding, or I'm shooting the shit outta all three of y'all freak asses. *Everybody* gonna be leaking!" Clay was infuriated, taking this violation personal.

"Noooo . . . nawww!" The trio didn't know whether to risk running and get shot in the back or take their chances and try to rush Clay. But in the meantime, Clay's clock was ticking, and Trinity, now back in "hood mode," was ready to attack.

"One, two . . ."

"Wait! Wait! Hold up!" Each stared down the barrel of the pistol.

"three . . . Hurry the hell up and decide. I'ma empty this thang," he swore as the countdown continued and his gun begged to be fired. "four . . . five. Okay, fellas, what's it gonna be? Who gonna go home without one?"

"Nawww," the pleas for mercy went on as no one on the deserted block was there to hear them.

Trinity wanted to cut all three of her attackers and let it be boisterously known. "I'ma slice all y'all shit off to the balls!" she ranted breathing hard.

Clay felt the young mother had been through enough and ordered her to go put the stroller in his truck. "You and the kids go chill out. I got this." Wanting to get some sort of revenge before she left it in his hands, Trinity dropped the metal to the debris-littered concrete replacing it with a rusty hollow pipe. Drawing back with all her might, practically naked, she struck both men in the face who had violated her, knocking them off balance. Satisfied after seeing blood gush out from their foreheads, she did as Clay suggested.

Sitting in the SUV, she rubbed the side of her throbbing head while peering out the passenger-side window. Only moments after watching Clay march the men behind a cluster of bushes in between two barely standing garages, Trinity heard a barrage of gunfire. Expressionless, her outta-the-blue hero emerged, heading toward the truck, strolling past the blue cargo van as if he had just stopped to take a piss. Bending down, he picked up her destroyed screen iPod, throwing it across a vacant field as far as he possibly could. When he got inside the truck, he then noticed a bare-assed Trinity sitting next to him, with her breast partially out for all to see. Getting back out, he opened the hatch. Next to a few bags of groceries he'd just bought was a red duffle bag. He grabbed an old pair of track pants and T-shirt he worked out in for the distraught female to throw on.

With no words passed between the two and the radio volume down on whisper, he drove around nearly twenty minutes, getting his thoughts together as the two kids in the back slept. Finally, he looked over at the young mother who was also silent, reflecting on what'd taken place and spoke.

"Hey, what's your name, anyhow?"

"It's Trinity."

"Trinity?" he repeated in question.

"Yeah and for real, I wanna thank you. This the second time you done had my back."

"We good, ma. As far as I'm concerned," he made sure she was looking him eye to eye, "this morning never happened, right? None of it."

"Right," she happily agreed, wanting nothing more than the entire thought of the episode to disappear from her memory. "It never happened."

"Okay, Trinity, where exactly you live at?"

"I stay on Fullerton."

"Fullerton?"

"Yeah, two blocks down from your spot."

"My spot?" Clay finally smiled—his first of the day. "What you know about my spot?"

"Oh, I'm sorry, I just meant—"

"Naw, I was just bullshitting," Clay grinned, winking his eye. "We good. It ain't nothing. What's your address so I can drop you and your kids off?"

After telling him her address, Trinity wanted to cut off into him about how much she always like him and wanted to get with him. Yet considering the fact he'd just seen one man banging her and another man's hookup in her mouth, she knew this wasn't the time or the place. Just thankful Clay had rescued her from God knows what was enough for the time being. Getting the stroller out of the backseat, helping her with the kids, Clay walked to the rear of the truck, opening the hatch once more. As she stood on the curb thanking him once more and promising to return his clothes once she washed them, Trinity felt her chances of being his woman fade even more.

"Here you go." He handed her a small-size box that looked familiar to her just as schoolteacher Lynn Banks, late for work again, drove by in a rush.

"What's this for?" Trinity asked, never getting something for nothing before.

"I saw the one my manz Whip blessed you with was smashed, so here you go. Take this one. It's a different color, but it's all the same."

Amazed at his kindness at that point, Trinity wanted her hero even more than ever. Before driving off, Clay reminded her that what went down in the alley was their secret and no one, not even Whip, would hear about it from her. He had her solemn word.

Clay

More than an hour and a half had flown by since Clay abruptly left the block. Returning with a slightly different attitude, he had a few bags of groceries in tow. Getting Dorie to help him, Clay gathered a couple of household items from the stolen Walmart truck, along with a 27-inch flat screen. Not even asking Dorie or Whip if the count was right and was business on point, he headed a couple of doors down as nosy Mr. Jessie from across the street watched his every movement like a hawk. Momentarily staring up at Mrs. Gale's window, he asked Dorie if she had gone anywhere. When he found out she hadn't, the two men climbed the stairs to what Clay calculated had to be the elderly woman's apartment door. Before he knocked, he had Dorie go back downstairs and tally up the money they'd made so far.

Clay returned twenty or so minutes later. Without so much as a single word in the way of an explanation to his crew about his newfound concern for the "old woman," no one dared ask, and he didn't volunteer. Listening to the cash amount and an update, he then took the money Whip had rolled up in a thick blue rubber band. In deep thought, he went to sit in his truck. Usually they waited to the end of the day to count up, but Clay was the boss, and if he wanted his money in all wooden nickels at four twenty-three in the morning, then so be it. It was his world—his way. After making a few phone calls, he rolled the window down telling his two next-in-charge cohorts he'd check them later and was once again out.

Clay paid off some trusted guys he often dealt with from the East Side of the city to remove the rapist city-issued van. He also needed them to dispose of the bullet-riddled dead bodies from the alley. He didn't want to run the risk of some nosy kids playing hide-and-seek have their innocence snatched away by the sight. Or a few scrap metal-seeking scavengers discover them sprawled out, pants down, shot in the manhood *and* right between the eyes. Clay was beyond emotionally drained and rightly so. Fighting a terrible migraine, he headed home, which was out of character for him. It felt like he was coming down with the flu, yet he knew that wasn't the case. It was his mental mind taking over. Over the years Clay had suffered from them. Always in a battle with his conscience and demons from his past, this time he felt no remorse whatsoever having had taken three human lives. After all, his latest victims brought death on themselves coming in "his neighborhood" doing as they pleased. There were consequences to doing that, and they paid the ultimate price—death.

As Clay drove, he couldn't help but to think back on the day "Uncle James," as his mother had him refer to one of her "special friends," kicked in the rear door of the lower flat they lived in. His mom had been seeing "Uncle

James" on and off for a few months. At first, he started off good in Clay's youthful eyes, just as every random man his mother would bring home did. He never tried to stay the night after loud sexing his moms. He always had McDonald's or Burger King in tow and had even paid for Clay to go on a school field trip. Good old "Uncle James" was a winner to him . . . until late one night.

In a deep sleep, Clay thought he was dreaming when he heard the thunderous sounds of someone kicking the side door, then the rear. Dragging himself out of bed, he wiped the sleep out of the corners of each eye. He thought it was good old "Uncle James's" voice screaming out his mother's name and calling her everything but a child of God. He was confused. Maybe he was still dreaming. Standing in the hallway not knowing what to do or say next, Clay soon felt his mother's hands on both shoulders. Roughly, she pushed him, urging him to go hide. Of course, he did as he was told. In a matter of seconds, Clay's life and mental were forever scarred.

After hearing his mother trying relentlessly to move what sounded like the small two-chair table across the kitchen floor, Clay heard one more final kick on the door. He realized it was the sound of the door crashing onto the kitchen floor. At that point, he knew for sure it was "Uncle James's" voice indeed. He was yelling. He was cursing. He was knocking things off the countertops. And most disturbingly, the man who once came bearing gifts had yoked up Clay's mother. He vowed she would never leave him and be with no other man. Clay was terrified and in tears. His mother was struggling to scream out for help, but her pleas were muffled. Knowing he had to come to her aid, eight-year-old Clay came out of hiding. Searching his bedroom for something to use as a weapon, he emerged back into the hallway, a huge plastic toy sword in hand. Running into the kitchen, he was prepared to do battle.

Entering through the doorway, Clay was stopped dead in his tracks. His jaw dropped, and his heart raced. "Uncle James" was on top of his mother. Panting while making grunting sounds, his pants were down to his knees. The smell of strong liquor mixed with the night air breeze. Clay stood motionless as he and his mother locked eyes. The young boy saw the pain on her face. After a few brief seconds, he made his move. He dropped the toy sword he was holding and grabbed a butcher knife out of the drawer. Without saying a single word, Clay planted the majority of the sharp blade deep into "Uncle James's" lower back. In obvious agonizing pain, he yelled. When the man, four times his size, fell over and off his mother, Clay ran over in the corner to grab a broom. Before he could swing the red-handled makeshift weapon, his mother was back on her feet. She took him by the hand, and they both bolted out the door to a nearby neighbor's for help. By the time the police had come to apprehend "Uncle James," he was long gone.

Years went by, and neither Clay nor his mother ever saw him again, which was good. Clay hated busters that strong-armed the pussy from bitches since that day. He had zero tolerance for that type of shit, which made it extra easy to do what he had just done back in the alley.

Not wanting to think about the memory of his awful past any longer, the sworn thug shook that shit off. Stopping by a soul food restaurant, Clay picked up a dinner to eat later and a bottle of Tylenol. Forced to constantly push IGNORE throughout the morning on his phone, he had about had it and was ready to change his number—again. Rhonda was relentless, not really knowing what she'd said or done to make Clay lose interest and was hell-bent on finding out. Whip texted him she'd come on the block more than three or four times looking for him since he'd left. Her drugged out Grandmother Ida was even with her once, running off at the mouth.

For the time being, Clay couldn't give a shit about Rhonda, Dorie, Whip, who had the best dope, the girl he'd saved from getting gang-raped, or the three guys he bodied because of her. He was headed to bed.

Chapter Eight

Nosy Neighbors

Well, after the block shut down and the dealers, along with the heavy flow of customers, had left, Mr. Jessie couldn't help himself. What he'd saw had been eating at him. Taking his job as Block Club president to heart, he wasted no time calling his longtime neighbor and friend, Thelma Gale. Considering the fact she was elderly and left to fend for herself most of the time, Mr. Jessie made her one of his top priorities when patrolling. Observing the main person who he knew was the boss, Clay, along with his worker Dorie, enter the building Mrs. Gale lived in, he'd waited all evening to invite himself over to her apartment to find out if she knew or had heard anything that would aid his attempts to shut the ill-mannered dope crew down.

"Sure, I'm still up, come on over," she cheerfully offered, welcoming the company. "I'll make us some coffee."

Before she could hang up the phone, stand up with her cane, and make her way to the kitchen to put on the coffee, there were two knocks on the door.

"I'm sorry to bother you so late, Thelma, but I need to ask you something. It's been kinda troubling me all day."

"No, no, I was up. I'm glad you called. Come on in while I fix us some coffee." Not being able to normally have enough for herself, let alone someone else, the fixed-income senior citizen was overjoyed having been blessed not once by whom she could describe as an angel, but twice.

Having been in his neighbor's home several times a month helping her bring in her groceries, care boxes, or serve as somewhat of a bodyguard to fend off the always-begging, predator-intent addicts, Mr. Jessie was stunned as soon as he stepped foot through the door.

"Oh my goodness, Thelma! What's all this?" Confused, he touched the DVD player that was attached to the fresh-out-of-the-box flat-screen television. "And all of this?" He nosily marveled at her countertop that was filled with everything from lotion and aspirin to mouthwash and cans of coffee, one which she had opened and was brewing in her new coffeemaker. "Where did this all come from?"

Not the least bit ashamed of her windfall, Thelma answered. "A new friend of mine blessed me with some things. Praise God."

"What—a new friend?" Mr. Jessie looked bewildered with raised eyebrows. "And did this new friend also mysteriously bless you with all these groceries I see spilling out of your cabinets as well? Those are not the brands of can goods and whatnot we give away at the church. I can see you have a lot of top-shelf items. Wow, things and your circumstances have suddenly changed, I gather."

Handing him a hot cup of coffee, Thelma reached for her new television remote, turning the sound down as she sat in her favorite chair. "As a matter of fact, he did. Why do you ask?"

"No wonder I didn't see you go to the Outreach Pantry this morning. The reverend was looking for you also. He saved you a box . . . even brought it over to my house himself. I set it right outside your door." He hissed in disgust and disappointment alike. "Wow, I knew something was strange when I saw you come home in a cab yesterday."

Thelma knew where he was going with the questions and quickly realized the true purpose of his impromptu visit. "I think I know what you're going to say."

Cutting his elderly neighbor off, Mr. Jessie went into his wannabe police mode. "Thelma, please tell me you haven't made friends with those street hooligans—those thugs down the street. I hope you haven't accepted these items as any sort of payment for your silence for all the crimes they're out in the street doing." Clearly agitated, he set his coffee down, fed up with what he now knew, or at least thought, was going on.

"Listen," with shaky hands, she placed her mug on the table beside his. "I don't know what you think but—"

"Thelma, was that thug over here today—in this apartment or what? Is this where he and that other one were taking that all that stuff to? Please tell me they haven't threatened you or tried to intimidate you. Is *that* what this is all about?"

"Slow down. No one has threatened anyone," she insisted with a feisty attitude. "You are the only person who has come in here yelling and carrying on. The boy was kind and polite. He talked to me with respect."

"Kind and polite? Respect? Is *that* what you call all these probably stolen items he has so-called blessed you with—respect? He and his posse are like cancer to this neighborhood! You look out the window every day. You see the madness they're causing. Hell, you were almost trampled the other day."

"That young man didn't cause me any harm. He was only being generous and helpful like the other day."

"Other day? What you mean other day? Just because that idiot stopped you from being knocked to the ground face-first he's some sort of hero, like my dead son, may he rest in peace? Is *that* what you're saying?"

"Oh my God," she pressed her hand to her chest. "Calm down, Jessie, please. I'd never compare him to your son. I know what tomorrow is too. I haven't forgot."

Mr. Jessie suddenly felt like he didn't know who Thelma was anymore. Harboring mixed responses of anger, sorrow, and regret hours before the anniversary of his only son's death fighting overseas, the father had zero tolerance for a man he felt shouldn't even be alive while his child was dead "Okay, Thelma, it seems like those criminals have somehow bamboozled your usually good judgment of character. I guess you wanna turn a blind eye to what they stand for, the crime they're responsible for, and the change in our once-quiet neighborhood."

"Of course not."

"Then explain all of this 'stuff' and your newfound tolerance of that low-life drug dealer! He and his crew are animals—homegrown terrorists!" The conversation intensified.

"You have it all wrong. But all your screaming and accusations are too much!" Thelma's soft-spoken voice rose. "Now, I've had just about enough, Jessie! I don't have to explain to you or anyone else my actions. He saw I needed help, and he stepped up and helped me; nothing more and nothing less." Her voice trembled as she spoke. "And, yes, I'm thankful to Clay. I don't think he's the monster you're painting him to be."

"Wow, so you two are on a first-name basis, huh?" Visibly disappointed, Mr. Jessie shook his head with contempt in his voice. "Well, just so you know, my police scanner first picked this up; then I saw it on the news. A Walmart truck full of merchandise was reported stolen and recovered a few blocks from here—broken in, stripped, and empty, of course."

"Really? A truck? Near here, you say?" Thelma, rendered speechless, puzzled, hoping the obvious wasn't true as her blood pressure skyrocketed.

"Yes, Thelma, right around the corner damn near. You didn't see it on this new fancy television of yours?" sarcastically he said, heading toward the door. "They say everyone has a price, but I didn't think a woman as strong as you are in the faith would be bought off so cheaply. Jesus help you, Thelma!" He made his longtime friend feel all the more guilty before delivering the final blow of insult and scare tactic. "And just so you know, receiving stolen property is against the law!"

Seconds after walking out of senior Thelma Gale's apartment, Mr. Jessie tripped over the cardboard box filled with food he'd set down by the door. Beyond aggravated, he pushed speed dial on his cell.

"Hello, yes, it's me. We need to talk."

Mr. Jessie

Swamped by various heartfelt sentiments all night long, Mr. Jessie, like his wife, awoke with mixed feelings of pride and sadness. Today, on the second anniversary of their son's death—or murder, as they often referred to it—they got dressed to visit the cemetery. Placing flowers on their child's grave at least three times a year—today was especially hard for the couple. Somberly leaving from their front door and walking on to the porch, Mr. Jessie and his overly emotional, distraught wife had no time or interest in what Clay or his cronies were doing or going to do. As far as they were both concerned, the thugs could have the block this one morning. Mrs. Jessie even forgot to snarl at the passing

Abdul and his little sister, what she did every chance she saw the pint-size Islamic soon-to-be terrorists that she felt were directly related somehow to the death of her military son.

"I wonder where they nosy asses headed to so damn early—probably a meeting for snitches! They probably take classes in that bullshit!" Whip's wild assumptions were followed by Dorie's on the early-morning crowded street.

"She got a Bible in her hands, fool, and it ain't even Sunday. Plus, she got some kind of stuffed animal or something." He couldn't help but notice Mrs. Jessie's overall sad demeanor and slow reaction mannerisms. "They're probably headed to a funeral or something like that—maybe a kid they know." Checking his cell for the time, Dorie suggested they get the block pumping before Clay got on set, or they'd mess around and it would be one of their funerals.

Momentarily watching Mr. and Mrs. Jessie wave at the old grey-haired woman from the building his once cold-hearted boss had taken such a sudden interest in, as well as the fake do-gooder Reverend Richards, who were both standing on the corner talking, Whip got to work getting the customers in line and the runners in place. Ida, feeling she was special and bigger than the game, shoved her way to the front beasting, even managing to elbow the schoolteacher, Lynn Banks, out of her cherished spot.

Seeing Ida instantly reminded Whip to try calling Trinity once more. Listening to Ida talk reckless about the size of their rocks versus the next crew and her irate granddaughter, Rhonda, complain about not being able to catch up with her self-proclaimed "man" the evening before had set his twisted thoughts and mind in motion. Finding out Clay had allegedly dropped his latest conquest and her badass kids off at her house and not even mentioned it to him caused Whip to be even more suspicious of Clay's outta-the-blue strange behavior. Whip wanted to flat-out ask him what the deal was but knew that would cause a major problem. Too many other out-of-the-ordinary things had gone down over the past few days in the hood. There was no need to rock the boat any further.

From where they came from and the number of females that were begging to just "be around," he had to appear to remain in total beast mode. Just having hit it, he definitely wasn't set tripping over the worn-out pussy, but was just curious. However, it was no secret to him or half the people standing around. Clay didn't like questions or those who asked them. Whip's only hope in knowing the true 411 was Trinity. Strangely, the desperate, thirsty-to-come-up female was all in the other night on his nut sac, but was now sending him to straight to voice mail, stuntin' like she was some sort of a G. He was no hood detective and definitely not on no spy shit, but in Whip's book, something wasn't right and didn't add up.

Clay

Spending a few minutes at the house he, Whip, and Dorie used to cook up in, Clay sat alone at the table going over the past couple of days' sales numbers. He was about ready to re-up and wanted to make sure everything was everything where his cash was concerned. Although he wasn't where he wanted to be as far as that went, the seasoned hustler was well within his goal. Pushing his chair back from the table, Clay stood to his feet. Suffering from another slight migraine, he rubbed his hand down across his face and soldiered up. It was time to get back to getting the rest of the money that was still out in the streets.

Deciding to leave his truck parked on the block a few houses down, Clay made the short hike to the spot on foot. He knew sometimes the element of surprise was better in business when you have employees. If they couldn't see you coming, they wouldn't have a chance to clean up or hide the sneaky, low-key shit they might be doing. Although he trusted Dorie and Whip, creeping on them both was how he was feeling today.

Bending the corner, he watched with a keen eye as runners made their way back and forth from the stash spot that they were forced to move daily, thanks to Mr. Jessie, who had just driven by with his wife in the car, and his secret squirrel wannabe-a-detective ass. In between him calling the law and Reverend Richards preaching against the dangers and downfalls of doing drugs, the entire crew had to stay alert and on their feet. It only took one day of lazy hustling in Detroit and you might fuck around and get caught slipping. And as of late, the normal numbers of police cruising by had increased. That increase made Clay order a "zero tolerance" policy on unneeded bullshit with his crew. It was now business first, last, and always when posted with the bag.

Less than two yards from the stop sign, he spotted the mouthy minister holding what seemed like an in-depth conversation with Mrs. Gale. Wanting nothing more than to speak and inquire how she liked her new television set, Clay felt it was best, like they had discussed the evening before, that they just nod to each other for the sake of keeping her good name just that—good.

"Hey, what up, doe, Rev?" he growled, barely acknowledged their presence as he walked by with an arrogant thug swag and a nonchalant tone.

"Hello. Good morning, son," Thelma couldn't help but reply as Reverend Richards nodded his greeting with both contempt and respect. She prayed the two of them would not come to verbal blows and wanted to defuse any ill thoughts of that.

Glancing over his shoulder, Clay gave the old woman a faint grin and a wink letting her know he was only playing the game and all was well. His apparent fake greeting was to just irritate the preacher. Not more than a few feet away, Clay could hear the so-called good reverend start browbeating the elderly Mrs. Gale about her unexpected burst of friendliness to a young, reckless dope dealer. As his ears filled with words no man of God should say about the next person, Clay felt his inner demon awake. He wanted to run over and open-hand smack the motherfucker for not only running his name down, but talking loud to the old woman.

Hating foul lame! He stealing niggas' bread every day and worried how the fuck I make mine. I should murk that pussy where he stand. He got me and my pedigree all the way twisted. If we wasn't out here getting this money, I swear to his damn God today would be that foul nigga's last, he angrily mumbled under his breath before meeting Abdul and his sister near the alleyway.

"As-Salaam-Alaikum."

"Wa-Alaikum-Salaam," Abdul responded with a huge smile. "I wanted to thank you for the other morning with those guys. It's like that almost every time they see us."

"I told you before, no thanks is needed. We good. Just watch your back. I just saw them around the way standing in front of the gas station."

"I hate those big yucky boys," the little girl frowned. "They're so mean."

"Well, I tell you what, li'l sis." Clay got on one knee so they were face-to-face. "If any of them mess with you or your brother again, I'll beat them up myself, okay? I promise."

"We should be good for at least the rest of this week. They all got suspended until Monday for stealing out of the teacher's purse," Abdul sighed with relief.

After reassuring them again that he was indeed 100 percent on both their sides, they parted ways. Clay had a drug empire to watch over, and the day was young.

Chapter Nine

The day went by practically uneventful as far as hood standards were concerned. However, anytime you hustled in the streets, flat-out street shit was bound to happen. Midafternoon, Rhonda showed up and turned all the way up, talking about this and that she'd heard about him and the ratchet girl down the way with the toss up babies. But Clay, trying to keep his encounter with Trinity low key, shut Rhonda down quickly, smacking her face damn near off her body for mouthing off to him. She's lucky she had the option to walk away on her own two feet and not get carried away by an ambulance—or worse than that, the city morgue. Everyone knew he didn't tolerate that nonsense, but she, like her grandmother, didn't think the rules applied to her.

When the commotion finally settled down, Clay sat on the top stairs of the flat staring from one end of the busy block to the next. Concentrating on how to make more money by stretching his product, his feet started to sweat in his boots. No sooner than he looked down to unloosen his laces and ask Whip for the latest count, he was met with the sight of Mrs. Gale making her way from the Outreach Building, cane in hand. Next to her, Reverend Richards was carrying one of his church charity meal boxes that most of the poverty income-level residents relied on—some even more than crack cocaine.

Not this con man again. Clay leaned back on his elbows, moving a toothpick from the left side of his mouth to the right, letting it rest on his lip. "Okay, Whip, what we looking like so far?"

"We ten down, three up, and two and a half in the hole."

"Okay, that's a bet." Clay shifted positions, acting like he wasn't paying careful attention to Mrs. Gale and the preacher. "We need to pick up the pace and get finished out here. Shit, I got a feeling the block might is about to get even hotter."

The closer the pair got, the antsier he became, hoping he could control his urge to pop off. When they were directly in front of the house, the reverend's cell phone rang. As he excused himself, setting the box on the bottom stair, Thelma took the opportunity to ask Clay how he was doing. Not caring about Whip and Dorie's facial expressions, he replied "good," standing up out of respect. Overhearing the reverend's one-sided conversation pertaining to a few missing city workers and their vehicle that was last dispatched in the vicinity, Clay coldly felt no remorse for their disappearance. They had coming what happened to them. And he would double kill them all over again if need be. However, he knew that any extra light being shined on the block he was selling at would be bad for business. As long as he had product on the block, Clay wanted if safeguarded. Most crackheads wanted to cop in peace and make it to wherever they wanted to take their blast in the same manner.

"Mrs. Gale, I'm so very sorry to be so rude, but this is my brother. You know, the one running for mayor," he proudly bragged for all to hear. "I have to get back to the church. He has a couple of news cameras on their way and—"

"No no no! Please, you go on now. I'll be fine." She didn't have to do much convincing as he briskly turned, headed back toward the church. "I can maybe ask one of these gentlemen to help me with this box that I told you

I didn't need in the first place." She didn't want to look a gift horse in the mouth, but the wise grandmother knew the reverend was just trying to be nosy and grill her some more about what Mr. Jessie had reported. Sarcastically, Thelma smirked, making her way to her own building just in time to take her medication and watch her mid-morning shows on her new television.

Clay had Dorie grab the small-in-size-but-too-heavy-for-an-old woman-with-a-cane-to-carry box. Without hesitation, no questions asked, Dorie took it up to the apartment door he and Clay had taken the Walmart stolen items to the previous day.

Whip was still confused from the day before when Ida and Rhonda came on the block mouthing off about old girl. Yet, he had tried all day to put it to the back of his mind and stay on his grind. Now, just like that, Rhonda's dick-crazy, good-stalking, not-wanting-to-take-no-for-an-answer ass had come back with more of the same. After acting like he wasn't ear hustling on the loud rants of Clay's jumpoff of the month, Whip waited until the count was low and his boss was seemingly distracted in deep thought. It was time to make his move and get some answers. Easing his way down the street, Whip felt his animosity grow with each swag-filled step. *Out of all this random pussy around, why this nigga knock this secondhand ho off and ain't say shit?* He got closer to Trinity's house as his mind raced. *I mean, like, damn, Clay, we could've both hit the bitch at the same time. It wouldn't be shit to it. But why perp? What's the big ancient Chinese secret about blowing her back out?*

A few more feet and he was at his destination—her walkway. Turning his baseball cap backward, Whip spit on the grass after seeing Trinity laid back in an old plastic white chair with one of the arms broke off with headphones in her ears. "Damn, girl, oh, your punk ass alive?"

"Huh?" With dark sunglasses on, she barely raised up removing the plugs. "What you say?"

"Oh, so we play the dumb role now, huh? Is that how we doing it these days?"

"Whip," Trinity, still feeling emotionally numb from the traumatic experience the morning before, didn't want or need any more problems. "I saw you was calling and texting me but—"

"But what, you ungrateful little bitch?" Whip wanted to play hard core, like shit didn't matter, but got caught in his feelings real quick, recognizing the T-shirt she had on. *I know this ain't that nigga shit this slut rocking—the one he work out in all the fucking time!* "You was too busy sucking the next dick to get back? Is that it?"

"Shhh . . . please," Trinity stood up begging him to keep his voice down before he woke both her sleeping kids. "It's not like that, baby, I swear. I'm just going through something right now."

"I bet you is." Whip snatched her cell phone up from the concrete banister. "Let me see what your green snake in the green grass been up to." After several tries, he realized he couldn't break her security code.

"What the fuck is you doing?" she tried yanking at his arm unsuccessfully reaching for her phone. "You think because you gave me a few dollars and an iPod you own me or something? You tripping!"

Whip stopped when Trinity said the word iPod, noticing the one she had was an entirely different color than the one he'd given her. He knew right then and there, besides Dorie, Clay was the only one that had access to that shade. "What's your code, ho?" His demeanor grew dark, wondering why the dude he was so loyal to would be so petty over some stanking rotten-smelling pussy. "What the fuck is it?"

Trinity was over trying to get her phone and finally gave in to his demands. "It's 6969—why? What's wrong with you? Why you need to check my shit?"

"6969? Figures, you dirtball." Infuriated, he pushed the numbers in sliding the bar over to the side while mumbling under his breath about the iPod and T-shirt. Once he got to her home screen, Whip slowly searched down her call log discovering no numbers belonging to Clay or any text messages from him either. "Here you go, slick ass. You probably erased the shit!"

"Erased what?" Almost missing catching her tossed cell, Trinity's sunglasses fell to the ground revealing the battered and bruised side of her face. "Urghh."

"What the fuck happened to you?" Whip blurted out, pausing with fake concern. "Damn!"

"It don't matter. I'm good." Trinity had enough of his verbal assault and sat back down. "Just leave me alone. In between you and that crazy bitch Rhonda earlier, I'm done!"

"Say what?" Whip tilted his head as if he hadn't taken in her words correctly. He was surprised hearing what he heard. "Dang—so if Rhonda was here, you already know we know what time it is—lying ass." He smirked with satisfaction. "I ain't know she had it in her."

"Just go." Uninterested in any more confrontations, Trinity threw her hand up not wanting to go into details of what Clay's supposed jumpoff had said to her or divulge the secret she was hiding from them both. "I'm not trying to talk. Just leave."

"Well, by the looks of your face, I can see Rhonda done got you all the way together, so I'm out. Do you, baby girl—do you. You lost out on some more of this here good dick and got an ass kicking. I hope he was worth it. And by the way," he stopped in his tracks showing her the rubber band grip handle of his pistol, "what's understood doesn't need to be explained but in case you slow, if you tell ole boy I was down here, your kids gonna be orphans by daybreak."

As Whip walked off the porch with a smug expression, Trinity let him believe what he wanted to believe about her bruises and her kitty kat. At this point, it didn't matter. He was just another dude she'd slept with who called himself set tripping. Keeping her word to Clay was all that was important.

Chapter Ten

"Fuck it! Let's shut it down." Clay rubbed his hands together taking notice of the near-vacant block. "We done did what we came to do." He manipulated his toothpick from one corner of his mouth to the next.

"Damn straight. Man, we did almost close to double with this new strong package," Dorie announced, going over the numbers in his head. "What you think, Whip? We hit them Twelfth Street busters in the head! This re-up was much better than the last shit they had."

Whip was still feeling some sort of way toward Clay but tried playing it off. "Yeah, y'all, shit was banging today."

After checking the stash spots and paying off the runners, the trio was ready to part ways for the night.

"You riding with us? I know you ain't walking back to your truck," Dorie assumed, even though Clay stayed strapped. "Not with all that bread on you. Niggas be thirsty as fuck!"

Clay stretched his arms glancing up at the old woman's window, then stepped back on the porch. He stood silent to gather his thoughts. He then decided to stay around a little bit longer to think. Nodding at the young Muslim boy and his family returning home from evening prayer at the mosque, Clay started to get a pounding headache. A lot of bullshit he was doing the last couple of days was out of character for him, and the block was the only place he could think. The streets raised him and always made him feel at home and welcome. "Naw, I'm good with it.

Y'all go ahead and break out. I'm 'bout to be here for a while—chillin'."

"Want me to stick around? Maybe I can call ole girl from the bus stop and one of her friends you can smash," Whip suggested with an arrogant tone and a twisted lip. "She ain't shit but a tramp anyhow. She'll be down with it!" Playing with fire, Whip kept pushing for a reaction.

"Dawg, I'm telling y'all, I'm straight. I'ma a real killer by nature. Nobody want it, for real. Go focus on some other shit in ya life." Clay felt himself getting slightly annoyed at all the low-key shade about Trinity Whip was throwing throughout the day and tried to bring it down a few notches before he blew up. "Look, Whip, you and Dorie go do y'all's thing, okay? I'ma in the zone and ain't trying to blow up the spot on no foul shit. I'm about mines tonight. Y'all already know how I get down. Just bounce—see y'all in the a.m. Go get y'all head straight or something!"

Knowing it wasn't in their best interest to argue with a grown-ass man, especially one with an anger management problem like Clay, Dorie started his car as Whip, hyper as ever, jumped in the passenger side. Seconds later, they were off the block and out of sight.

Twenty minutes or so went by. Leaning back on the wooden stairs of the abandoned house next to the stash house, Clay heard a sound of breaking glass. Not sure of where exactly it'd come from, he stood up. *What in the fuck?* Seconds later, he heard an echoing sound of what he believed to be a door being kicked. Gun in hand, he eased off the stairs, slowly making his way around the side of the house creeping into the backyard. After making sure his own immediate surroundings were secure, Clay headed back up the driveway toward the porch.

Before reaching the second side door of the two-family flat, the young hood warrior saw a series of lights click on, then off in the house across the street. *Is this what the hell go on when we shut down?* he pondered, watching nosy Mr. Jessie's windows like a hawk. *I know good and damn well niggas ain't being reckless! Not on my block—making the shit hot!*

Having been posted all day, Clay knew the man always trying to throw salt in his game and his wife were still out somewhere, yet to return. To reassure what he already knew, the couple's car was absent from the driveway of their home. Sure the lights could've been on some sort of timer—but then that thought was pushed right out of his head. Tucked in the darkness of the night, he witnessed what looked like at least three or four different people scurry past the upstairs and downstairs windows and peek out the front curtain of the door. Not knowing just how many there truly were or if they had guns, Clay quickly ran back to the rear porch retrieving two more pistols his runners kept stashed—just in case.

Upon his return, adrenalin pumping, he was met with Mr. Jessie and his wife getting out their car. "Yo," Clay tried being discreet, not wanting to alert the burglars inside before he taught them a lesson for disrespecting the block where he made his bread. "Hey, yo—over here, old man!"

Momentarily slowing down, the emotionally drained couple both noticed the otherwise bloodthirsty drug dealer that would normally let them both burn to death without so much as taking a piss to put them out took notice he had guns in both hands. Not wanting to fall victim to the ever-present swelling crime wave that Detroit was famous for, the pair rushed to the porch before Clay could warn them.

Damn! He now had to figure out what to do next seeing the overly cautious wife and Mr. Jessie closing their front door, unaware of what was awaiting them on the other side. Looking up once more at the old woman's window, Clay darted into her building and up the stairs, taking them two, some three, at a time. Wasting no time, he banged on Mrs. Gale's door hoping she, unlike her neighbors, would trust him enough to see what he wanted before passing judgment.

"My goodness," she didn't hesitate unlocking several deadbolts for the young man who had become her savior of sorts. "What's wrong? Is everything okay?" she asked, holding her housecoat tightly seeing he had guns in his hands.

"I hate to bother you, but this is important. You know the man and woman across the street?" Clay ran over toward the window, peeking out through her curtains. "The ones who drive the black car with the rag roof?"

"You mean the Jessies," Mrs. Gale was starting to get nervous as well as confused. "Of course I know them— been knowing them for years now. What's this about? What's going on? Son, why do you have those guns? What's happening?"

"Listen, do you have their phone number?" Clay glanced over his shoulder long enough to make eye contact her, then went back to focusing on the lights that were now all on in Mr. Jessie's house. "I need you to call them and see if everything's okay. Can you do that please?" His breathing increased, observing the shadow of what appeared to be someone getting shoved around through their blinds.

"Please, Clay, they don't mean you any harm." She replayed all the horrific atrocious things Mr. Jessie, along with the good reverend, had been telling her about him all day. "I'm getting scared. Please! I'm sorry—you can take all this stuff back but please don't hurt them."

Clay knew then and there, no matter what he did or said, he was labeled a monster in her sight and always would be. But that was the title he rightly earned in and around Detroit and had to deal with the consequences that came with it. "Okay, listen, Mrs. Gale," he watched her clutch her Bible to her chest. "I think someone broke in their house." He shrugged off her misconceptions of his murderous intent, staring back out the window.

"Oh my God! No! We should call the police!"

"Look, I was gonna go handle it myself before it got to this, but they came home." Clay finally turned back to face the old woman he'd grown strangely fond of. "That's why I need you to call over there. I think, naw, I *know,* your friends done walked in on they asses! Ain't no telling what's going on behind them doors. And as for calling the police—even if you did—you know this is Detroit—they ain't coming for at least two hours *if* they show up at all!"

Thelma knew what he was saying about the police was true and wasted no time dialing her longtime neighbor's phone number which she knew by heart. Getting no answer the first time after letting it ring ten or eleven times, she tried again. Sighing with semirelief, the old woman finally heard the sound of Mrs. Jessie's shaky voice say hello. Having been coached by Clay to just act normal and see what was what, she soon got the feeling Clay was right—something was seriously wrong in that household. Never having been rushed off the phone before by her friend, the conversation grew more random as the moments passed. "Wait now before you hang up. I just wanted to ask if you had any coupons for Tide detergent."

While Mrs. Gale attempted to keep an elusive Mrs. Jessie on the line, Clay stood posted in the window, infuriated and pissed about what was now taking place on his block. *Ain't this a bitch! Not these young, reckless motherfuckers again! I'ma give they crackhead mamas something to do Saturday morning, fucking with me and my cheese.* Recognizing one of the always mouthy teens he'd had a run-in with at the corner store, it became painstakingly clear what the small, inexperienced group of petty thieves were now caught up in. What they probably intended on being a simple burglary of a television, DVD player, and some jewelry had now become a home invasion, and by the looks of the youth marching Mr. Jessie from the rear of the house to his car, a kidnapping charge was not far behind.

"Keep her on the line as long as possible," Clay whispered heading out the door into the hallway with both guns still in hand and another securely tucked in his waistband.

"What if she hangs up?" Mrs. Gale looked worried and distressed. "Oh my—then what?"

"Then grab that Bible of yours over there and get to praying 'cause somebody gonna to meet they Maker tonight!"

"Hey, yeah, it's me, Whip."

"Why you calling me? What you want?"

"What you mean what I want?"

"You heard me! I'm done playing all those fake games from earlier."

"Look, girl, just meet me at the damn Coney Island, okay? I wanna holler at you."

"For what, Whip? What we gotsta talk about so damn important?"

"Look, crazy bitch, I'm done with this phone shit—is you coming or not?"

"If I'm there I'm there; if I'm not, then so be it."

"Then that's on your slick-talking ass!" Pushing the red button on his cell, Whip then filled his boy in on his plans no sooner than Dorie finished pumping gas at the CITGO Station. "Hey, Dorie. You can drop me off on the next corner. I got some bitch business to handle in a few."

"Your crazy ass must be about to hit old girl off again." Dorie shook his head, turning the car's engine on, pulling out into traffic. "Well, I hope your ass be in a better mood tomorrow than you was today, 'cause for a minute, I thought you was gonna have Clay fuck around and get on ten!"

"Yeah, dude. That no-wall-having rat been blowing my shit up all fucking day begging a nigga to come tear her thang out the frame." Whip blatantly lied, jumping out half a block from the restaurant. "And FYI, Clay ain't the only one that can get on ten! You must've forgot how a nigga like me gets down when pushed. I make boss moves when need be. I goes all the way off. Remember that drought and money was tight?"

After stealing a Jeep from the employee parking lot at the local college, Whip and his forever-loyal comrade Dorie hit I-94 heading east, putting the Hemi in the engine to work. As Dorie drove, Whip went through the owner's glove compartment and center console hoping to find some petty cash or possibly a credit card. Finding nothing of great value, he reclined the seat for the short-distance ride they were taking. After twenty minutes or so, they pulled over at the mall, parking the car in far corner of the lot so no one would notice the broken steering wheel column. Going into one of the main entrances, they didn't stop to window-shop as they exited at the far end, easily finding another vehi-

cle to steal. Back en route to their destination, Whip followed the same routine in that car as well. Coming up empty-handed again after searching that glove compartment and console, he frowned. When his homeboy slowly turned into the parking lot of an out-of-the-way jewelry store in a not-so-crowded strip mall, he was back on alert. As they drove past, they noticed the showroom was empty of customers.

Momentarily seeing no one was coming in or out of the adjacent stores, the pair inconspicuously slipped on their mask. With hammers in their back pockets, they quickly exited the car, leaving it running and the doors unlocked. Within a matter of seconds, the wild, ill minded pair was inside the normally tranquil confines of the store. As a shocked staff hurried to mash the alarm button, the showcase glass was shattering, and Whip and Dorie were grabbing their hearts' desires of rings, chains, and watches, putting them in plastic bags. Just as fast as the masked hooligans had entered the building, they were gone. Jumping back in their second stolen car, they roared off and were soon back in the first one on I-94, home bound.

Before they could get back in the neighborhood good, Whip shot a move over a random female he was kicking it with. She had been blowing up his cell since the moment they'd stolen the first vehicle, and he wanted to set her straight. He wanted to teach her the life lesson that no ho strong sweated his balls. As Dorie stood guard on the girl's front porch, Whip savagely beat her to sleep—almost permanently. When she regained consciousness, he had left her one of the stolen diamond rings. Whip and Dorie still laugh how the desperate bitch still be on his line.

Chapter Eleven

Easing his way across the eerily quiet block he normally ran with an iron fist, no fear, no second thoughts, Clay boldly walked up Mr. Jessie's empty driveway. Standing close to the side of the brick wall in the darkness his anger grew. *These little fuck boys gonna learn today!* Sweaty palms on both guns, he looked back toward Mrs. Gale's dark apartment getting a glimpse of the religious elderly woman peeking from behind her lace curtains serving as a Bonnie lookout to his Clyde. *She better get that Bible ready!* With the silence of a mouse and the heart of a lion, he perched down under an open window. Posted up, he was listening for any sounds of voices that would tip him off exactly where the young thugs were located in the dwelling that they so dumbly chose to take over. And most importantly, Clay needed to know where the innocent Mrs. Jessie was.

Listening to the cruel loud commotion of household items and keepsakes being broken, smashed, and thrown around, Clay made the decision that he'd heard enough and waited long enough. Mrs. Jessie's desperate pleas for the wildin' out teens to "please just leave" and "don't hurt me," along with the constant disrespectful names they were calling her was working the drug dealer's last nerve. *Oh, it's on!*

Taking several deep breaths, Clay got into his "by any means necessary" mode. Cracking his neck from side to side, he was seconds away from going all-out Dexter-

Linwood Comanche style inside the back door that was still cracked open—both guns blazing. With one foot on the bottom stair and the other still on the ground, he suddenly saw the beaming glare of headlights pull up into the driveway shining in the backyard where he was at. *What in the fuck!* Assuming it was Mr. Jessie and the self-proclaimed leader of the gang returning, Clay hid behind the thick rosebush hearing both car doors shut and footsteps getting closer. *Okay, wannabe grown motherfuckers! Let the games begin!*

"You broke-down, expired, old crazy man," the teen aggressively shoved Mr. Jessie in the small of his back with what he claimed to be a pistol. "What kind of bank only let you get a measly punk-ass $300? I should kill you in this backyard. Then go kill that ugly mugged wife of yours in there with the big booty; the same one my boys probably fucking the dog shit outta right now while you busy out here running your mouth."

"I swear to God if you or those thugs hurt my damn wife!"

"*What if we do?* What the fuck you gonna do? Not jack shit. You straight pussy!"

"Listen, young man, please, let us be. Please. You're not gonna get away with doing stuff like this. You all gonna end up in jail one day!" Relentlessly, the Block Club president tried negotiating his and his wife's freedom from the living nightmare they were in. "Why don't you kids get jobs or something? Go to school—I don't know what's wrong with your generation!"

Amused at the things Mr. Jessie was saying, the inexperienced-to-real-life criminal-minded adolescent was preoccupied with returning his own brand of opinions on his and that of his cohorts' lifestyles. With his back now entirely turned to the in-full-bloom rosebush where Clay was hiding, waiting to pounce, he pushed the older man up the stairs, causing him to stumble, falling on one knee.

Clay knew this was the opportunity he was waiting for and rushed out, ambushing the boy half his size. With force, he snatched him up off his feet, squeezing his forearm tightly around the teenager's throat. Smashing the side of his handgun onto the side of the youngster's temple, he immediately knocked him out cold as a startled and confused Mr. Jessie looked on. Using the barrel of the other gun, he winked, placing it up to his lips, signaling for Mr. Jessie to be as quiet as possible and creep back down off the stairs.

With callous intent and his blood pressure sky-high, he quickly dragged the slumped over, now skull-busted youth around the rear side of the garage by the boy's thick, freshly braided cornrows. Clay then trustingly took his chances doing something he never ever did before—gave a civilian to the street life a gun with his fingerprints on it—especially one that he knew fact for sure had bodies on it.

"Here, guy, take this nine in case this little bleeding pussy wakes up. And if he does before I get back . . . well, that's on you to decide."

Dried mouthed and at a total loss for words, Mr. Jessie wasted no time taking the firearm from the infamous NFL4LYFE-tattooed drug dealer he'd been trying to get arrested and locked up for years. Within a blink of an eye, the always-law-abiding citizen was now faced with the possibility of participating in vigilante justice of a wounded person. Now truly being faced with being judge and jury, the emotional night had just reached another turning point. Shaking with fear, he didn't know what he'd do to the unconscious, pint-size menace if he woke up and tried to get away, the one who'd slapped his wife twice and spit in her face before making him go to the ATM and withdraw money from his savings account . . . but time would soon tell.

"Look, dude, just stay back here and chill. I'm about to slow walk them other little bastards out here with this crack baby." Clay kicked the boy who was lying facedown on his stomach in the side of his ribs, but he still didn't move.

"My wife," Mr. Jessie's eyes grew twice their regular size with anxious worry about his better half. "She's still in there—with those monsters! I've got to help her! We gotta call the police!"

"Pump your mind flow, Block Club Prez. Around here, *I* am the police! I got you and her!" Speaking in a low tone, Clay held the man's shoulder back talking him down from trying to be a hero. "Just don't call no cops while I'm in there! Let me handle this! I got this!"

Bewildered, not knowing if Clay was directly working with the misguided group of hooligans or not, Mr. Jessie had to trust him in hopes that he would see his loving wife alive again. With no cell phone, trying to get help from a neighbor, or call the police—who had the worst response time in the nation—would be no use. Time was definitely not on his side. As he watched Clay take another pistol from his waistband and cautiously enter the rear of his home, his heart raced with anticipation over what was gonna happen next.

Two guns posted at his side, Clay slipped his muscle-chiseled body through the open doorway entrance into the kitchen. Careful not to make any noise, he overheard the ill-bred youngsters in the front room. In their own warped world discussing who was gonna get what and how much cash they hoped their boy was gonna return with, Clay, sneaking up on them, was the last thing on their young selfish minds. With the whimpers and sorrowful cries of Mrs. Jessie coming from a closed utility closet located off what had to be the basement stairs, Clay exhaled, glad she was at least out of harm's way of what he had in store for the talkative misfits.

On a mission of mayhem and revenge, Clay continued through the strawberry-melon, candle-scented home with one thing—and only one thing—in mind—making the out-of-pocket crooks-in-training pay in full for stepping on his toes. Everybody and they mama in a ten-block range in each direction knew Clay had a strong grip on the various streets he hustled on and didn't tolerate any sort of bullshit—especially shit that involved officers of the law or even the dogcatcher being called.

The fact these basic-acting Negroes violating his strict hood-inspired commandments were legally underage meant absolutely nothing at this point in time. It was unmistakably on. If they wanted to run buck wild with the big dogs, with no collar or leash on, then there were consequences—some fatal. The game was the game, and they chose to break the rules. Justice would be swift.

"So, y'all punks think this madness is gonna fly, huh? Terrorizing old people." Clay surprised the three peers of the sucker he'd left stretched out on the side of the garage leaking from the head. "In *my* damn neighborhood? Seriously, on *my* fucking block? Come on now, I know y'all knew better than that!"

"Aww, shit." One jumped to his feet while the other two scattered to the far corners of the living room. "Clay, Clay, we . . . umm, we . . . ." He stumbled on his words, wishing he was anywhere but in this room with a gun aimed in his face.

"We *what,* nigga—huh, what? What you wanna say now, big man, before I put a few of these hot lesson-learners up in ya? Y'all smart-asses need a li'l lead in y'alls unde-veloped diet anyhow." Clay grinned holding both .40 cals extended out in their direction, eager to pull the trigger. "Y'all should know I don't operate like this. Didn't I just warn you little bitch-prototype-fools the other morning about disturbing the goddamn peace around this moth-erfucker?" He gave them a cold dark stare as if he was *daring* one of them to contradict a single solitary word of what he was saying. "Y'all wanted to be about that life—well, hello, fag one, two, and three—you *are* now!"

"Dude, please!" Damn near in tears, the smallest of the trio begged, dropping a DVD player to the carpeted floor as he pissed on himself. "We was just messing around. We ain't even wanna come in here—I swear!"

"Ain't no passes on this right here! Now, I'ma advise all y'all to get over there on the floor." Clay pointed one gun near the beige-colored La-Z-Boy recliner, tucking the other in the spine of his back. "And hurry the fuck up before I have y'all bleeding the hell out like y'all's boy who think he so damn tough!"

As each boy started crying, begging for mercy, Clay felt no remorse for what he was planning. He knew there were too many of them to just body, so he had to think of another way to make them pay for their transgressions of the block. Yanking one up by his collar, Clay raised his arm, crashing it down with brutal intent, sending his victim to his knees. Smacking the crying wannabe tough thug across his barely grown mustached lips with the gun's handle, Clay laughed out loud seeing the other boys' reactions. Shoving the muz-zle to teen's chin, slowly nudging his head backward, the predator-motivated-group had now turned to prey. Clay ordered them to all sit down while he held his own style of street court.

Suddenly, Clay's rant was halted. The ear-deafening sound of a single gunshot rang throughout the sparsely populated neighborhood, echoing off the walls of the abandoned homes. Assuming it came from the backyard area and Mr. Jessie had "handled his business" and pulled the trigger, Clay gave the three boys he was now holding hostage a stay of execution from his wrath. "Gimme all three of y'all fucking cell phones! Now, I'm gonna have the names, numbers, and ugly-ass pictures of everybody y'all li'l bitches run with—just in case!" After letting them know he knew where they went to school, where they laid their heads, and the fact that he'd hunt them down and put a bullet not only in their brain but their mama, sister, and great-granny as well if they tried to retaliate, he let them go out the front door unharmed.

Heading back through the ransacked house, Clay unlocked the utility closet. Having heard the gunshot also, a hysterical Mrs. Jessie burst out, practically knocking Clay to the ground.

"No, oh my God! Oh my God!" Frantic, she screamed out, trembling in fear of what had happened to her soul mate. "What have you done to my husband? Where is he? Oh my God!" Beside herself, she focused on the large shiny pistol in Clay's hand, naturally believing the shot she'd heard from behind the shut door had harmed Mr. Jessie. "Oh my God! Noooo! Where is he? Where? What have you done?" Terror ensued. Searching the kitchen with her eyes for the young black-hearted captors, then looking up the hallway toward the living room, her anxious pleas got louder. "Where is my husband, you monster? What did you do?"

"Wait, miss, wait! Slow down—damn, slow down." Clay threw up both hands trying to calm her fears, letting her know the worst was over. "Your husband is okay. I promise you—he's good. Lower your voice with all that, lady—he's good! I'm trying to help you!"

Watching the local drug dealer she'd see every day flooding the neighborhood with cocaine stand in the middle of her kitchen claiming that all was well, Mrs. Jessie felt light-headed and sick to her stomach. She wanted to throw up. She wanted to scream and fall to her knees. Confused, fighting through the dizziness, she made a mad dash bolting through the still-open back door to get help. Before she could reach the bottom stair, the distressed woman locked eyes with her husband who was standing over a body with what appeared to be a handgun lowered at his right side.

Getting closer, the half-out-of-her-mind wife saw a look of desperation and shock on her husband's face. Throwing her arms around his neck, she waited for him to hug her back, but he didn't. She begged him to raise the mysterious gun he had and protect them both from Clay who was headed near them, but he didn't. Mr. Jessie stood almost motionless and deaf to her cries. As Clay walked up on the couple, Mr. Jessie finally spoke, barely louder than a whisper, staring down at the moaning-in-pain youth.

"He was moving, trying to get up," he mumbled as Clay took the pistol out of his hand. "I didn't know what else to do. I swear to God, I didn't. I thought he might . . . I . . . umm . . . What did I do?"

Mrs. Jessie's cries became silent, realizing Clay was telling the truth. Her husband was indeed alive, and Clay was trying to help them.

"Look, I already told you, I got this," Clay insisted, placing the gun in his waistband. "This wasn't on you, old man. They brought that bullshit to you and your wife! This *wasn't* on you. I mean, I know y'all heard about them little kids and them three other people they found dead in that house down the way. That could've been you and your wife on the news next; dead as a motherfucker. You did what you had to do; bottom line."

"I know but—"

"Look, you was only protecting what is yours! Ya feel me?" Clay didn't want any cops being called, although the always-nosy neighbor seemed to be heading down that path. "Hey, y'all just go back inside the house, lock your doors, and act like this never happened." He bent down, grabbing the injured teen by both legs, flipping him on his back. "Why risk being arrested and fighting a case on some shit that wasn't even your fault? Why waste lawyer fare on a little nigga that was gonna probably kill you *and* her! But that's on you—my hands clean! If you wanna risk jail time and use your once-a-month check on a lawyer—then make that call!"

"But—but—" In a daze, Mr. Jessie's mouth grew increasingly dry in denial over what he'd done—the act he'd committed. "I don't know—"

"Well, *I* sure as hell do! He's right," the man's wife strongly urged, pulling her man back toward the stairs she'd just fled from. "Those thugs were going to kill us both! I heard them talking," she panted out of breath, glad to be alive and talking. "Don't go to jail for them. Don't let that miserable thang lying over there win."

"You better listen to her and just forget about it." Clay nodded to Mrs. Jessie, seeing they were on the same page. "Trust me, this piece of rotten shit lying here or those little crab motherfuckers that bum-rushed your crib ain't coming back—never! Let it go! I done told you—this ain't on you! None of it!"

After being at the cemetery and coming home to this horrific aftermath, the Jessies were mentally beat and their faith utterly tested. As the overly emotionally drained couple disappeared into what was once a safe haven to them both, Clay dragged the now unconscious teenager down the litter-filled alley. When he got near a vacant garage packed with debris, he tossed the half-dead teenager behind an old piss-stained mattress. Going through his pockets, Clay took the badly injured teen's cell phone, just like he'd done his cronies.

Before going to his truck which was parked a few blocks over, and calling it a night, he walked past Mrs. Gale's building so she would know all was well with him. He owed his "lookout" at least that much. Without slowing his pace, Clay smiled up at the elderly woman's window, seeing her standing there, clutching her Bible closely.

Chapter Twelve

Reverend Richards

"Yes, do you have any idea, Reverend Richards, what is the reason for the spike in crime in Detroit—especially District 5? It's almost at epidemic proportions—on the brink of organized chaos!"

Trying to seem as confident and loyal to his brother who was running for mayor as possible, the man of the cloth took a deep breath before responding to the cocky news reporter. "Well, you have to remember, sometimes it's not the number of crimes committed in a city that's the problem; it's the overall leadership. That's what you have to take a look at."

"So, sir, are you insinuating that our current mayor and his various appointees are failing to provide adequate protection and/or solutions to the citizens? Is that what I'm hearing? I mean, we were just out here speaking to your brother the other day, and he seemed optimistic about working with the current administration, even during this election year."

Confidently straightening his necktie, he leaned into the microphone that was only inches lower. "What I'm saying is that if something isn't working properly, it might need to be replaced or upgraded. Don't you think you deserve better? I deserve better? And the good, long-standing, law-abiding citizens like the folk I have standing behind me deserve better?" The Outreach

Building's pastor pointed back to Mrs. Gale and Mr. Jessie, both of whom he had to practically beg to come to the impromptu interview. "Even these little ones going to school deserve better!" He noticed Abdul and his little sister who were walking past all the early-morning commotion.

"Well, Reverend, are you saying the mayor is supposed to be some sort of Superman? I mean, what exactly can your brother," the investigative reporter eased in for the kill, "or any other candidate have done to stop the mysterious disappearance of the three Water Department employees, the apparent hijacking of the Walmart truck recovered a few blocks over from this location, or the disturbing discovery just this morning of yet another teen suffering from gunshots, who is likely to be crippled the rest of his life—if he lived . . . found yards away from this food pantry? This district is totally out of control. And unless you been somewhere with your head underneath a rock, I know you've seen the news about them two babies and three other people discovered bound and gagged." He cocked his head to the side in anticipation as he continued his full-blown barrage. "Do you personally think the mayor and the police department can stop all this open-air drug trade that's going on in just about every neighborhood in town, or has it gone too far? Do you think Detroit needs the National Guard or martial law initiated? Has your brother shared his view with you?"

The usually talkative reverend seemed to be frustrated and at a loss of words as the high-energy journalist bombarded him with cold hard facts of multitudes of illegal activities that had taken place, and were continuing to occur—questions he didn't have the appropriate answers to.

Full of accusations, finger-pointing, and coming short of playground name-calling, Reverend Richards, power hungry in his own right, in one minute in front of the bright lights of the cameras, was on the verge of destroying all the positive work his half brother, candidate for mayor of Detroit, had built. Full of regret, Mrs. Gale, balancing her weight on her cane, and a solemn-faced, guilt-stricken Mr. Jessie, lowered their heads upon hearing the terrible but true crime statistics of the District 5 neighborhood they all called home—some transgressions they even had firsthand knowledge about.

Hotter than a cast-iron skillet of dirty fish grease and extremely embarrassed, Reverend Richards now sat in his private office licking his wounds. Having been tongue-lashed by his older brother and his brother's campaign manager for even speaking to the media about anything other than his own church business without their prior consent, the preacher schemed, wanting nothing more than a chance to save face with not only his sibling, but the public, as well. Caught deep in his emotions, the left side of his head started to pound. Swallowing two Extra Strength Tylenols, washing them down with a small swig of dark liquor he kept locked in his bottom drawer away from his sometimes nosy parishioners, the reverend closed his eyes.

"The block is off the chain today—hot as a mother-fucker," Whip made mention as he and Dorie drove past a group of people gathered in front of a huge camera propped up on a white man's shoulder. "No wonder that nigga Clay called and said to hold up till later. He got that third eye on the streets! We'd mess around and get knocked for real today!"

"Yeah, true that," Dorie agreed as he drove slow enough to stare down the block they made the most money on, yet fast enough that the certain packs of always-waiting heads didn't see them and cause a rush, drawing unwanted or needed attention. "Let's just go grab some breakfast and let that circus clear out."

"No doubt." Whip leaned back, thinking about the single gunshot he'd heard echo throughout the neighborhood last night. It was just minutes before seeing the same disrespectful wannabe gangsta group of teenagers, minus their mouthy leader, bolt past him and ole girl he'd met at the restaurant. He was still feeling some sort of way about Clay, but let it go for the time being. "Well, whatever jumped last night, the shit probably gonna be all on Facebook, Instagram, and Twitter. If Black Informant ain't talking 'bout it, then you know damn well the hood is. Them reporters was out there heavy."

Shaking his head, Dorie laughed, pulling up in the last spot in the lot turning off the engine. "Yeah, the motherfucking police ain't gotta earn they money no more. These social media snitches doing they job for free. If a fool get got at eleven, by midnight it's all across the Web."

Chapter Thirteen

"Good evening, residents of Metropolitan Detroit. The bloodshed and body count continue to rise tonight. I'm here on Fullerton Street between Linwood and Dexter Avenue, which is located on the West Side of the city. Sadly, tragedy has once again struck our economically stressed and crime-infested town. After several frantic 911 calls were received, police burst down the doors of the home located just behind me." The reporter pointed up toward the yellow-taped-off house as a crowd of shocked neighbors gathered around. "What they found behind those doors, no one, including many veteran officers with as much as twenty years on the job, could stomach. The victims, three young adults, were found brutally murdered, two of them bound and gagged, and one seemingly killed execution style. However, what makes this crime scene more heinous and heart wrenching than the other breaking news homicides we've reported on this evening is that, unfortunately, there were two other victims, both elementary school-age children." The angry, concerned crowd continued to grow as the lights from the camera shone bright. "Our sources tell us both small children were found duct taped together in a chair and possibly poisoned. The older of the two boys also appears to have been beaten. Identities are being withheld pending notification of families. But joining us live, we now have the newly appointed Detroit Police Chief Thomas Craig, who has just arrived on the crime scene. Chief, what can you tell us?"

"Yes, well, um, it has indeed been a night, or should I say a day of complete chaos in Detroit. Within a short 24-hour span, we now have at least seventeen confirmed homicides and more than nine or ten shootings that have resulted in minor non-life-threatening injuries. Our prayers go out to all of the victims' families, and I also want to reassure our law-abiding citizens that the department is working overtime to regain order and diplomacy on the streets." The chief then gave a long cold stare into the camera dead-on as he made his point clear. "These criminals will not take over our city! These savage, senseless acts will definitely not be tolerated, and those responsible will be apprehended and swiftly brought to justice. All available manpower has been called on duty, and no stone will be left unturned. I'm putting everyone breaking the law tonight in Detroit on proper notice: We'll be coming for you in full force."

A group of elderly neighbors clapped as the camera continued rolling and the reporter shoved the microphone in the chief's face, holding him there. "Thank you, Chief. One last question. This has proven to be the deadliest day in Motown history. Do you have any suspects in any of the crimes as of yet?"

"At this time, all leads are being aggressively followed, and we encourage the public to contact us with any information that will assist in our efforts. Thank you."

"Well, there you have it. The chief has assured us he and his officers will restore peace to Detroit. Live on the West Side, Jayden James reporting for Channel 7 Action News."

Less than an hour later, after watching the constant rebroadcast of the tragic news reports, Whip and Dorie were finish devouring their grits and eggs breakfast.

Before leaving the restaurant, the pair plotted out exactly how the rest of the day would go if they hoped to make up for the lost morning-shift revenue. With a sense of determination, the two headed back toward the block. Elated and relieved to find the unwanted hood visitors had vacated, undoubtedly back to the tranquility of their own neck of the woods, huge grins graced both their faces. Finally, it would be business as usual. Gathering all the runners who hadn't disappeared searching for other hustles for the day, Whip and Dorie retrieved the half-sold package they'd stashed from the night before. As soon as the dope was almost at point zero, they'd hit Clay for the re-up.

Most of the morning custos had probably gone across the way to their competition to cop, but the ones who wanted that good strong blast Clay was famous for putting out in the streets—waited. Passing out a few testers and two-for-one specials to let the word get out they were back up—the money started to flow. Rubber banding three racks of crumbled twenties, dirty singles, tens, torn-corner fives, along with a few big face hundreds, Dorie eagerly placed the call to his boss.

Chapter Fourteen

Reverend Richards felt a little light-headed from the combination of the aspirin and the liquor. Knowing he had to at least get some information to pass along to his brother about how the district could reduce the crime stats, he looked into the mirror, getting his game face on. Unlike any of his soapbox sermons to the underprivileged or giving out, supposedly, no-strings-attached food rations and clean clothing to the drug addicts, he knew he had to come all the way correct if he wanted to get what he needed to save face in the family and community. The man of the cloth needed a miracle from a higher power— one that had more clout than God in this district. There was only one person in the neighborhood that possessed just as much, if not more, control and influence over the downtrodden residents than the man upstairs—and that was Clay. And Clay, cut from an entirely different cloth from the others, needed the good reverend for absolutely nothing, so helping him would definitely not be a priority.

With a false sense of entitlement, he made his way down the block in search of the local drug kingpin of the vicinity. Trying to appear unmoved by the news reporter's verbal attack from earlier, he knew was probably the talk of the hood, so the reverend worked to keep up his fronts. As he walked by the two Muslim kids he always gave shelter to when need be, he loudly warned them to be careful because one of their known tormentors had been callously beaten and later died the night before, and was discovered only yards away on the side of a dilapidated garage. Under his breath, he advised them to come directly to him if they had any information about the crime. With a hard heart, he let the kids know if they even thought about not telling him every single detail they might overhear at school or anywhere else, he might be forced to tell their father, who was an overly strict and devout Muslim, that they had been seeking refuge in the church—even reading the Bible.

Promising a few of the nosy seniors extra food boxes later and giving crackhead Ida some spare change if she took her begging on the other side of the district line, the self-appointed, one-man, crime-cleanup guru then made it his business to approach the same well dressed woman in the silver Toyota Corolla he'd see every morning parked at the edge of the street near the stop sign getting high. Informing her one of his loyal parishioners had copied down her license plate at his request, Reverend Richards seemed to take pleasure threatening exposing her to the Federation of Teachers if he saw her anymore "disrespecting" his community. Before the scared-to-breathe woman pulled off, he made sure to question her faith and spirituality, almost damning her to hellfire himself.

The closer he got into the thick of it all, Reverend Richards looked for the comfort of any familiar faces—but saw none. From porch to porch, curb to vacant lot, astonished, he watched the local dope boys darting in between houses and fields serving customers in broad daylight as if the drug trade was legal and a dead body wasn't just found hours earlier. He knew Clay and his team were hardened by the way they carried themselves on a daily basis, but to be so nonchalant about a boy's death that was nine outta ten times a friend of some of theirs was strange. The neighborhood he once loved and cared about making a change in was gone. Drugs and crime had taken over, and he could only shake his head, knowing he was also part of the problem. The preacher's hands were not without the blood of the downfall. He knew better than try his "save the hood" act on them, so he kept it moving.

Finally at the spot Clay made his makeshift overseer refuge, he took a deep breath. Anxious about the reaction he'd possibly receive asking to speak to the drug lord face-to-face, the minister once again looked for his neighborhood favorites for mental strength and an extra pair of eyes—just in case. However, Mrs. Gale was mournfully tucked back away in her apartment, Bible in hand, asking the good Lord for guidance, knowing she'd taken place in serving as a lookout for what had ultimately turned into the high-publicized murder of a troubled teenager. The elderly grandmother tried to call a couple of her own children for advice, but, as usual, her calls fell upon deaf ears.

As for Mr. Jessie and his wife, he was suffering from his own firsthand grief, knowing he'd pulled the trigger, putting at least one hot slug into the youth's body, while his better half was feeling no sort of remorse whatso-ever. She, in fact, was infuriated beyond belief she, her husband, or even "badass Bobby Johnson" Clay hadn't had the opportunity to kill the entire shameless group of hooligans that'd violated her home—one even disre-spectfully urinating on her deceased military son's flag that had once proudly draped his coffin. At this point, she was mad at God for letting the whole ordeal jump off in the first place and warned her husband, Mr. Jessie, about feeding the reverend any more so-called anonymous tips about Clay's comings and goings and other activities, let alone him standing behind him at the press conference.

***

"Yeah, old man! What up, doe? What you need?" Whip was being a smart-ass, cocking his head to the side as he spoke. "You trying to get on or what?"

"Fall back, guy, I got this." Dorie stepped up, quickly intervening before things got out of control. "What's the deal, Preacher? The old lady up in the building and your people from across the street ain't out pretending to sweep. So what's up? You trying to get on? You trying to get high? Or you out chasing behind some of this young pussy out here?"

"How you two young men doing today? I didn't come to see either of them, well, not today, anyways." He ignored their insults and accusations of illicit intentions.

"Look, Preach, cut the dang formalities short, all right? What you need from us? Why you down here on our end of the block?" Dorie snapped, cutting him short. "What's the deal?"

"Well, um . . . um, I was trying to get in touch with Clay. Is that possible?" He glanced around not seeing him. "Me and him need to talk. It's important."

Whip laughed at the man, who was known to call the law on them each and every chance he got. "Y'all need to talk? Aww, man—no, you didn't. Come the fuck on with all the bullshit. What y'all got to chop it up about, huh? Is you about to give us the schedule that the damn police gonna make they rounds—with your good-snitching ass? Take your miserable ass on somewhere else."

"Look, son, it's not like that," the reverend proclaimed with a straight face.

Once again, Dorie came in between the one-sided heated exchange, trying to maintain a straight face. "Okay, dude, he ain't here. But whenever I get up with him I'll be sure to let him know that y'all need to talk. So for now, you can just bounce!"

"Yeah—be gone," Whip snarled just as Clay's truck bent the corner with the re-up. "Go save some damn souls or some of that shocka locka magic voodoo y'all be doing."

The block grew amazingly still as Clay slowed down, brazenly tossing a brown paper bag to one of the runners to hand off to either Dorie or Whip. As he parked in front of Mrs. Gale's building entrance, he glanced up but didn't see her sitting in the window. Refocusing on the surprise visitor that was standing near the stoop, Clay made his way toward the house as heads and kids alike begged for money before being chased off by an agitated Whip.

"What's all this?" Clay frowned, skeeting a thin stream of spit through the side of his clenched teeth. Staring at the screen of his ringing cell, he shook his head. "Yo—why my streets looking slow? Y'all li'l niggas need to be out here picking up the pace before you be looking for work elsewhere!" Arrogantly, he walked past Reverend Richards like he wasn't there. "Y'all out here holdin' church and shit when y'all outta be getting my paper." Like a ghetto king, he commanded his soldiers while he took his seat on his concrete top stair throne.

"Excuse me, young man," the reverend fought to get a word in edgewise.

"Y'all heard my manzs," Whip yelled before disappearing in between two vacants to stash the new package. "Let's get this shit back pumping hard on they asses," he reemerged, extra hyped.

"What's the count?" Clay eased back on his elbows as the summer sun bounced off his unlaced Tims. "How we looking?" He kept shooting anonymous calls on his cell straight to voice mail. He'd been getting them ever since he turned his phone back on and was annoyed.

"We good money," Dorie replied as the reverend tried getting closer to Clay before being physically blocked by Whip, who was looking for a reason to show out. "Ain't no problems but this irrelevant old man."

"I said, excuse me, Clay, but can I speak to you for a min-
ute or two? I was telling your people—it's kinda important."
The reverend put on one of his fake scheme-worthy smiles.
"I just want to talk!"

"You wanna talk to me?" Confused and not giving a shit
at the same time, Clay spit over the rusty steel railing.
"Well, talk."

The uninvited guest paused. All eyes and ears of
the street were on him. He momentarily had the floor.
Reverend Richards was used to being the center of
attention behind the pulpit in front of his devoted congregation, but this was a command performance for the
streets filled with the people that hated him the most. At
this moment in time, Clay was Jesus Christ himself, and
he was viewed as the devil burning Bibles on a Sunday
morning on the church stairs. "It's something we need to
discuss in private, young man, if you don't mind."

"Maybe he wanna talk about being down the way
fucking with our customers and shit," Whip hissed,
folding his arms with attitude. "Yeah, guy, I seen your
fake scripture-quoting ass all up in the window of that
uppity bitch car—or was you just trying to get your old
dick sucked?"

"What?" Clay acted as if he hadn't heard correctly. "Is
that right—my custos?" Whip got his boss's total attention. "He fucking up my money flow with my people—I'm
sure he don't want us to run up this Sunday fucking up
his bread. That bullshit can go—just—like—that."

"Son, wait, it's not like that," Reverend Richards tried
unsuccessfully explaining and defending his actions but
got shut down.

"Yo, you calling me a liar?" Whip blurted out, ready to
pounce. "That's the shit I don't like, so what's good with
that?"

"We can trade words all day, son, but, no, it's not like that," he bargained.

"Y'all can't trade shit all fucking day on my damn clock, and you, rat-style nigga, it's like this." Clay sat up, tired of the verbal games being played. "Do I bring my black ass down to that pimp game church of yours talking about I wanna talk to you in the middle of a damn sermon? Hell, naw." He then stood to his feet not waiting for a response as his voice grew louder and the veins on the side of his temples seemed to be popping out of his skin. "Or do I come down there interrupting you passing out them rotten fruit, expired-canned-meat welfare boxes? Once again—hell, fuck, naw! But you down here wanting me to stop doing my thang because all of a sudden—*you* wanna talk. What's the occasion?" He rubbed his chin, smiling with contempt. "I thought you did all your talking to the damn cops or maybe that news reporter that clowned your media-thirsty ass this morning."

Reverend Richards was second guessing what he'd gotten himself into. He had no clue what Clay and his henchmen were capable of. He was dry mouthed because as much as he hated to admit it, he had no defense. He did have a relationship with the police, and the reporter did ambush him. And he was out of order for expecting Clay to just bow down to his wishes. Throwing subliminal threats to get his way certainly wasn't gonna work. "You know what, son, you right! And when you right—you right," he conceded, praying to calm the situation down before he got jumped and stomped. He remembered what had happened to Reverend Wianns a few months back at the gas station and wanted no part of that type of possible treatment. "Well, if you can find time at the end of the day so I can have your ear for a few minutes, I'd appreciate it. I'll be at the church until at least ten tonight."

Not accepting or declining the impromptu invitation, Clay turned his head in the other direction, focusing on his money. The reverend didn't hesitate. He wisely took that as his cue to exit.

Chapter Fifteen

"Thelma, I need you to try to talk to that wild boy. This district is out of control, and you know good as I do, Clay is behind most of the madness that goes on around here. He got something to do with the dead bodies, the drugs, the stolen merchandise, missing people—you name it, that monster has got his hands in it somehow."

"Listen, Reverend, I told both you and Mr. Jessie, I don't have any power over that young man." She peeked out from behind the curtain watching Clay argue with an unruly girl. "He's not gonna listen to an old lady."

At his wit's end, Reverend Richards poured himself another stiff drink. Taking two, maybe three, swigs, he started to reveal some hard-core truths he recently found out about Thelma. "Well, you have some sort of favor from that thug judging by the stolen goods in your apartment. And please don't try to deny it."

"What?" The elderly woman stared at the black screen of her television, then her new coffeemaker. "I can't believe you're saying that to me, Reverend, after all the years I stood by you and your ministry. Where is your Christian compassion?"

"Yeah, well, if you don't want the entire Detroit Police Department kicking in your front door and hauling you off to jail for having all that Walmart stuff," his voice started to slur as he blackmailed the senior, "then I strongly suggest you get him to show up before I leave for the night. I'll be in the Outreach Building until ten."

"Are you serious right now, Reverend? I can't understand or believe what you're saying to me. I would be
lying if I said I was not in shock. You would call the police
on me?"

Reverend Richards gave his longtime parishioner and
supporter a devilish grin before answering. "To be honest
with you, Mrs. Gale, yes, in a simple heartbeat. So, it's in
your best interest to do as I ask—or get ready to do some
serious jail time. And at your age, that may be a death
sentence."

"These fools these day be doing way too much." Whip
shrugged his shoulders. "I don't see how they stay alive."

"Yeah, that was some crazy shit. The minister trying
to talk all of a sudden," Dorie replied, easing Clay his
money. "Bugged out!"

Seconds after getting his bread, a still extremely
focused-on-the-block Clay was thrown off his square.
Rhonda, her sister, and some random bitch pulled up like
they were the police. Jumping out of the passenger seat,
Rhonda was clearly double caught in her emotions. She
got loud with Clay for the third time in four days since
he'd cut her off. Running reckless at the mouth about this,
that, and the third, she professed her loyalty and undying
love for Clay. With her ghetto-minded crew standing off
to the side of the curb watching and waiting for his reaction, they could see the steam rising from Clay's body,
even if Rhonda could not. Trying to negotiate with her to
get back inside the car wasn't working. Even though he'd
smacked her down to the pavement the last time she got
out of line, Rhonda was intent in wildin' out. He tried his
best to not nut all the way up, but Rhonda was begging to
get hurt, both physically and mentally. She was seconds
away from getting what she showed up for.

"Yo, nigga! I know you hear me talking to you, Clay. Why you doing me like this?" She tried tugging at his arm as he stared off into the distance. "What in the fuck did I do to you? Why you tripping all of a sudden? Why? I keep leaving you messages, and you just like fuck me like I ain't shit. That's bogus as hell."

Clay was about done in the patience department. His normal personality didn't call for allowing anybody say anything to him at any given moment, so today was out of the ordinary. First, the church Negro from down the block had his once-in-a-lifetime shot—now this worrisome bitch. While the customers, Rhonda's crew, and his workers alike looked on wondering what was going to pop off next, suddenly, it did. Clay, without warning, reached upward. Roughly snatching Rhonda down to the bottom stairs by her throat, he never changed his expression. Tightening his grip, the more pressure he applied, the more color seemed to leave her face. "Look, you little nothing-ass tramp, I done warned you about coming around here trying to mess up my money. Now, you back over here on the block like fuck me. Like what I say don't mean jack shit." Saliva spewed from his twisted lips as Rhonda's eyes started to bulge out of their sockets. "You keep blowing up my motherfucking phone like you don't get the point. Bitch—I'm done with your needy ass. What part of that don't your thirsty self understand?"

No longer on the curb, Rhonda's sister and friend were near the stairs. They were begging Clay for mercy in hopes that he'd let Rhonda go before actually killing her. Each cried out, promising they'd make sure she didn't come back anymore. Clay was no longer in the mood for negotiations. That window of opportunity was closed. The situation had become beyond explosive. Knowing the police might also show up at any given second, it was a high-alert moment. With the Block Club president walking his wife to her car, Dorie also urged Clay to free the relentless female. But Clay wasn't moved. He had been pushed over the edge and to his limit with the disrespect Rhonda kept showing.

"Naw, Dorie, this slut think I'm some sort of a joke. I'm out here doing what I do, and she think she got some special pass to come around this motherfucker like I'm a bitch. Hell, fuck, naw. It ain't gonna go like that." He finally let go, but not before smacking Rhonda up. As she fell back with a split lip and a face full of tears, Clay felt no sympathy. He then attacked once more. "I don't owe you shit. Now, I swear to God if you bring your punk ass around here anymore—it'll be your last." Raising his boot, he brought it down, cruelly stumping her hand before returning to the top of the stairs like it was nothing.

With three broke fingernails and two swollen, bloody knuckles, Rhonda struggled to breathe but was still caught in her emotions. "Naw, naw, he ain't right. He ain't right."

"Girl—damn, shut the fuck and get the fuck on before shit really get extra for your ass." Whip gladly came from across the street ready to clown. He was already off his leash from earlier. "You out here messing up our flow over some dick. You ain't got no clue what you about to get yo'self into. Now, ole boy said bounce—so git."

To add insult to injury, while Whip was practically skull dragging Rhonda by her weave to the car, ironically, Trinity bent the corner. Walking down the drug-infested block pushing her kids in the stroller, she had no choice needing one of the reverend's care packages that included baby formula. The closer the young mother got up on the obvious commotion, the two females locked eyes. The tension was so thick you could cut it with a knife. With scratches on her face from her and Rhonda's previous encounter, Trinity had the heart of a lion. The fact she immediately saw she was outnumbered meant nothing. If Rhonda wanted to go for round two—then so be it. Win, lose, or draw, it could be on. It was what it was. Plus, Trinity knew Clay wasn't gonna let jack shit happen that bad to her or her kids in his presence. He'd proven that in the alley. Their bond was unspoken but understood.

"Aww, hell, naw. Not this tramp, low-life, ghetto-style slut. Let me go. Fucking let me go."

"Look, Rhonda, leave that girl alone and get your black ass in the car before I fuck around and really lose my temper on you again *and* these hoes," Clay shouted off the stoop as Trinity slowed down, getting braced for whatever.

"Oh, so y'all fucking, huh? Is that it?" Rhonda fought to get away and at Trinity. "I already beat that ass the other day. You want some more, bitch?"

"Whip, get this skank ho off my block." Clay ignored the accusation as both Rhonda and secretly, Whip, waited for his response. "Matter of fact, from this point on, it's a bounty on this trick's head." With his chest stuck out, he stood to his feet like a king holding court. "Any of you young trappers out here want a come up? If you do, here's the deal. If y'all catch this broke, good dick-slurping, nothing-ass female on the block and kick off into her ass—it's a rack for each broken bone you bless the bitch with."

Hearing that, Rhonda got herself together and back in the car before the hungry runners took their boss up on his more-than-generous offer. "Bitch, I'ma see you out in these streets real soon—trust," she shouted to a still-silent Trinity as her girl skirted off the block.

Trinity was noticeably unmoved by the idle threat. Clay smirked. He was impressed by Trinity's ability to hold her peace no matter what the next female said to her or about her. If he wasn't sure if she'd stand tall about their little secret, he was now. She didn't flinch. Even when Whip started following her halfway down the block talking cash shit, she held her own.

Chapter Sixteen

Trinity Walker

"Why ole boy taking up for your punk ass so hellava?" Whip grilled a still-walking Trinity as if she was his woman or significant other. "Why he trying to save your ass from another beat down, huh? Why? Why the hell is that?"

Trinity wasn't in the mood for any more confusion of any sort. Her mind was still reeling from the worst dramatic encounter of her young life. And dealing with a jealous, apparently ex-girlfriend and a dude she gave the pussy up to one time wasn't on her agenda of important shit to do. She just wanted to pick up the food box with the baby milk and get back home as quickly as possible. "For real, Whip, I don't know why that nigga do or say what he do. Why don't you ask him instead of keep running up on me like I'm wifey or some shit like that? Damn."

"I'd never wife a slut like you. You ain't nothing but something a nigga fuck on when he ain't got shit else to do." Whip got in his emotions as he slowed down his pace. "You just got some good head on you, that's all. You just good for sucking a nigga dick until it throw up in your mouth."

"Well, if that's all I'm worth to you, what's the problem? You had all of that, and you still mad. I'm done entertaining this conversation, and for real, it's see you later. Bye."

Left standing there speechless, Whip allowed Trinity and her kids go on about their business. Caught up in his feelings, he went back down the block to see what, if anything, Clay was gonna say about the girl he seemed to be taking so much interest in.

Being asked by Reverend Richards to stand over to the side, Trinity felt uneasy. With things in her life being so financially stressed, the young mother often did what she had to do to survive. Trading pussy for food, money, or clothing was nothing new to her—but it was her choice to do so. Reverend Richards always seemed to undress her with his eyes and always held her hand extra long when greeting her. Trinity was far from being a fool. She knew given the time and opportunity, the supposedly God-fearing man would be just like every other man, with the exception of Clay, and take advantage of her neediness.

After everyone was gone, Trinity leaned up off the wall. Leaving the stroller off to the side, she asked the Reverend if it was at all possible if she could have a little extra formula because she didn't intend on coming back out for a while. Surprised by the smell of what she thought was liquor on his breath, Trinity eased back. "If it's not too much trouble, I'd appreciate it."

The reverend had an all-too-familiar, to Trinity, devilish grin. Recklessly looking over each shoulder, he boldly moved closer to the young female he often mentored about being overly promiscuous, telling her she could get anything she wanted if she just "asked the right way." The smell of liquor escaping out of his mouth grew stronger and stronger. The closer he got in her personal space, the more she searched the area for any of his usual nosy parishioners—but saw none. Time and time again, he'd tried to push up on her low key—but this was much different.

Besides a drunken Ida stumbling by, rolling her eyes on her granddaughter's behalf, and the Block Club president's wife driving by, that end of the block was practically deserted.

"Yeah, I saw you talking with one of those dope boys a few minutes ago," he stated in an extremely judgmental tone. "Is that the type of man you want around you and your kids? Did he do *that* to your beautiful face? You know he only wants one thing, don't you? Most men his age only want you for your body. I mean, seriously, what else do you have to offer?"

"Umm, we were just talking—that's all. Is that a crime or something?" she firmly placed her hands on both hips, sucking her teeth. "And, no, he didn't touch my face. Why would you even say that?"

"Well, even if you and he haven't done anything yet, it can happen. Talking to his type can only lead to one thing and one thing only—sex." Reverend Richards licked his lips like a cat about to pounce on a mouse. "Now, is that what you want, Trinity—sex?"

"What?"

"Come on, now. You remember what you told me happened with that other young man trying to abuse your child. You only need to have one good man around your children."

"What! Why you bring that up? I told you that in confidence, not to throw it up in my face."

"I'm just saying, Trinity. I didn't call Child Protective Services on you like I should've done, did I?" He rubbed his hands together as if he was plotting. "See, I'm in your corner. I can keep a secret for people I trust."

"You a minister, and like I said, I confided in you. But I see how it is now." Trinity was fed up with going through the word games he always played. She could respect him more if he just came out and said he wanted to hit it. "So look,

Reverend, can I have the extra formula or not? I have to get back home. I don't have time today for all that extra stuff you talking about. And matter of fact, truth be told, I don't appreciate it at all."

Realizing she wasn't gonna play his game, he felt it was in his best interest to just let her go. As bad as he may have wanted to let his man pride take over his thoughts, he stopped. The liquid courage he had made him overly frisky, not flat-out stupid. And the louder Trinity was getting wasn't worth the possible trouble it could cause. If she was caught in her emotions about the statements he was making to her, then she would play that game alone.

"Here you go, my dear. I didn't mean any harm or to offend you." Looking stupid, he handed her a fully stuffed box, adding a few more bottles of formula just as she asked. "I was only trying to advise you on this wicked world you are out navigating through. This neighborhood is an increasingly dangerous place. You know they found a teenager dead this morning, not too much younger than you. I know you probably heard folk in the street talking about it, right?"

"Yeah, right, whatever, Reverend Richards—whatever you say." She practically snatched the box, placing it underneath the stroller seat. "And, naw, I ain't heard nothing about nothing. I mind my own business around here, and maybe you should start doing the same thing." Storming off, Trinity had no idea the boy killed the night before was the one with all the mouth that had smacked her on the ass at the bus stop, but even if she did, she wouldn't give a sweet fuck anyhow. That was his mother's bad luck of a high-price bill to pay for a funeral and his bad luck for getting himself killed in the first place.

Mr. and Mrs. Jessie

"I don't know what to think of that sneaky preacher you so hell-bent on being in cahoots with." Mrs. Jessie took out some more cleaning supplies she'd just returned with. "It was bad enough you went down there this morning at that press conference, not knowing what could've come from it, but now he keeps calling you, wanting you to keep a special watch on that boy over across the street." She got back on her hands and knees trying to scrub out huge stains the group of scandalous teens had made. "If it wasn't for that boy over there—drug dealer, girl beater, or not—we could've both been dead like those people on Fullerton Street, not to mention you could be arrested."

"I know that, dear; trust me, I know," he strongly agreed, ignoring yet another call from the pushy reverend trying to get a minute-by-minute update on any news of the teen's murder so he could spoon-feed it to his brother. "It's just I don't want to cut him off cold, just like that." He snapped his fingers. "It might appear suspicious to him."

"Suspicious or not, I been telling you to cut that religious con man fool loose for months. Just because he loaned us money for the new roof a few years ago doesn't mean anything. You paid him back in full, plus he had me making free cakes and pies for the church every week, not even offering to reimburse us for the ingredients."

"I know, dear—you're right." Mr. Jessie had been listening to voice mails ever since this morning, pressuring him to find out "something" or he might let it slip out to his wife he'd been sneaking off to the casino when he was supposed to be at crime prevention meetings. "He only wants to get his brother elected; he doesn't care who he throws under the bus to do it."

"I know I am," she angrily huffed. "You don't owe him anything. We have to look out for our self!" Getting off her sore knees, Mrs. Jessie approached her husband and longtime companion looking him dead in the eye. "Besides all that, I just saw that old fool trying to lean all over in that young girl's face." She shook her head with contempt. "Is *that* what y'all do down there at that building half the night acting like y'all trying to fight crime? Having young girls in there doing God knows what?"

Reassuring his wife that wasn't the case and he'd avoid the reverend as much as possible, he grabbed some rags and started to help her clean. *Why doesn't he leave those young girls alone? One day he's gonna go too far. I warned him the last time he got the deacon's daughter pregnant and she threatened to tell if he didn't pay for the abortion and give her half of the week's collection. As the days go, by I wonder more and more if he's even fit to lead a band of church mice, let alone people. God help us in the days moving forward with him at the helm.*

Chapter Seventeen

Darkness soon took over the turmoil-filled day. Every customer was served, every dollar was counted, and every worker was paid. Long after the street was vacated, Clay noticed the glow emanating from Mrs. Gale's apartment. Having not spoken to her from the night before, he felt it was in his best interest to make sure all was well. Mr. and Mrs. Jessie were definitely on board when it came to remaining silent about the wild teen's unfortunate but very deliberate demise; however, when it came to the old woman, Clay had to make sure she understood what had taken place—had to. He had no idea if one or both of her longtime neighbors had confessed what truly jumped off at their home, but he would soon find out.

Within five minutes of Mrs. Gale letting him into the living room, he explained to her what really went down at the Jessies', and surprisingly, in the long run—she understood.

"Look, trust me, no one wanted to hurt that boy," Clay spoke in an even tone. "But if I start letting any-old-body, especially teenagers, run wild around here, ain't no telling what would become of this block."

"I know, but to see his family crying . . ."

"I know it was probably hard for you, but truth be told, it was either that little badass nigga that was terrorizing everybody around here with his crew or your people across the way." Clay pointed out the window. "Maybe you should call them and ask them if I did the right thing."

Mrs. Gale was at a loss. "No, son, it's not that."

"Well, listen, they had guns on them people, so if he wanted to go for bad, that's the route he chose—not me!" Revealing more of the details, he urged her to collaborate with her neighbors and verify his story as fact.

Taking him at his word, she then revealed to the young drug-dealing menace who had affectionately taken to her, Reverend Richards had threatened her freedom. She told Clay that if she didn't "make" him come to talk to the so-called good Christian pastor, that the police, along with his wanting-to-be-mayor brother, would investigate all the items he'd blessed her with and more than likely arrest her.

"I don't want to go to jail. Why would he say those things to me?" Her eyes started to water as the thought of the reverend's words resonated throughout her mind.

Clay was livid as he reassured her that set of circumstances would never *ever* take place. "Don't worry about anything," he said. "He a snake. What kinda man try to get tough with a damn old-ass lady—no offense, ma'am." Clay had blood in his eyes and fire in his heart. "I'm on my way to holler at him right damn now." Feeling the vibration of her apartment door frame shaking as Clay slammed it shut, Mrs. Gale started to read her Bible in hopes of calming her nerves. No more than into the second verse, she heard the bottom door do the same.

"Let me get this motherfucking straight. Your bitch ass had the nerve to call yourself verbally strong-arming an old-ass lady?" Clay wasted no time cornering Reverend Richards near the rear exit of the Outreach Building where he'd caught him. "Let me find out you trying to run shit your way around this bad boy, and they gonna discover your bitch ass laid the fuck out in the middle of rush-hour traffic somewhere. Now do me and you understand each other—or what?"

"Arggg, wait, wait," he fought to catch his breath and break free from the young man's certain death grip. "I didn't threaten Mrs. Gale. I swear I didn't. Where did you get that from?"

"Oh—so now she a liar, huh? Is *that* what you saying? The old woman is a damn liar?"

"Listen, son, I just wanted to talk to you—that's all." He dropped the small bag of garbage he was about to toss into the Dumpster. "I didn't mean any harm or any disrespect to her or you. I don't wanna have any problems between us."

"Damn—I thought we had an understanding about you fucking with my people."

"Whoa . . . So Mrs. Gale is your people now?" The so-called man of the cloth was being sarcastic, thrown aback at what he was hearing but not really surprised.

"Don't worry about who people she is . . . Just worry about what can happen to you and yours if you get at her again spitting that rah-rah bullshit. I don't give a damn about you or your wannabe mayor brother. He can get the business too for fucking with her. From this point on, she's off-limits." Clay let go of the man's neck while shoving him into the concrete wall in one swift motion. He was fed up and wanted to get to the real point at hand for his roughhouse demeanor yet anticipated visit. "So, look, old man, I'm here. You wanna talk and shit, then here's your only chance to do so. Now speak!"

Straightening his blue and silver necktie, Reverend Richards suggested they go into his office for some privacy. Not scared of what he'd find on the other side of the church doors, Clay obliged.

"Son, I'm not here to judge. You have your way of life, and I have mine." He nodded over toward a Bible. "Even God and the devil were friends at one point, so I know we can make a deal."

"A deal? Me and you?" Clay was puzzled and kept his eye on the shady minister. "What kinda deal would I wanna have with you? I gotta hear this bullshit."

"One that's beneficial to both of us."

"Beneficial?"

"Yes, sir. I get what I want—which is a slowdown in crime in this district."

"And?" Unmoved by words, Clay waited for the true punch line.

"And you get what you want."

"And, okay, old man, I'll fucking bite! What exactly is it that you think I want?"

"To sell your drugs in peace and stack your bread, as you young folk say."

"Is that right?" Clay walked around to the other side of the desk not knowing if the preacher was taping him or not. "I don't sell drugs—point-blank period!" He coldly stared into the preacher's face letting him see the handle of his gun. "That bullshit is illegal as fuck. A nigga a mess around and catch a case that way."

"Okay, okay, right. I understand. My mistake," Reverend Richards wasn't in the mood for round two of Clay's hands wrapped around his throat. "Let me rephrase what I'm trying to say."

"Yeah, you do that." Aggravated, not knowing where this meeting of the minds was going, Clay stepped back, looking at the time on his cell. "And hurry up, I got places to be. Time is money in my world."

"Son, all this, should we say . . . random victim crime is out of control in this district."

"Okay and . . ."

"And stolen Walmart trucks, missing Water Department workers, and dead teenagers' bodies turning up can't keep flying unnoticed by the local police or the federal authorities."

"What all that got to do with me? What the fuck you trying to say?" Clay knew where the preacher was going but had no intentions of traveling down that road with him—at least not willingly. "I'm about to cut out. I ain't come here for all that crime and police update shit."

"Calm down, son, trust me," he advised, eager to politic. "I'm not your enemy. We have more in common than you may think. Just sit back and hear me out. That's all I ask."

By the time the awkward summit was over, the two men with two entirely different agendas had astoundingly come to an agreement that was indeed beneficial to both. Deciding to somewhat join forces to the greater good of furthering each one's ultimate goal and outlook for the district they conducted business in, each felt the other had received the shorter end of the stick.

Chapter Eighteen

Clay

Clay, his crew, Dorie and Whip, met extra early to cook up a new strong package. After having Hustle-Man instead of Ida's pesky ass come by and do the testing, they were ready to hit the block. With a new attitude and game plan in mind, Clay gathered all the runners together for their new assignments and a heads-up on how things would be run from now until further notice. The entire operation was getting an overhaul.

"Okay, y'all, listen up. From this point on, I'm putting down a 100 percent zero tolerance when it comes to bullshit crime in this district." He took a long swig of a bottle of water, then continued.

"Huh?" a few of the guys wondered out loud.

"That's right. No fucking crazy-ass crime is to be going on around this motherfucker." Clay paced the floor holding court. "No stealing petty shit outta people garages. No breaking car windows because some asshole accidently left some spare change in their ashtray. No kids jumping on each other or stealing outta Sam's store up there."

"Man, Clay, how we gonna control all that? Niggas gonna be niggas," Whip laughed, elbowing a confused Dorie. "Especially in Detroit!"

"That ain't my damn problem how you do it." Clay stood still scanning the room with authority. "Just do it. Make my word fucking law—y'all understand? Spread the word."

"Okay, Clay, okay, relax. I'm all over it. Don't worry, I got you," Whip agreed, realizing his boss was serious as two back-to-back heart attacks.

"Good. And I got another news flash. Starting tomorrow, we doing shit different. We moving the whole hookup on both corners to the south side alleyway."

"Say what?" Whip was again surprised hearing Clay's additional plans for the first time alongside of the workers. "Damn, dawg, how custos gonna get thru all them bushes and shit? I don't think—"

Momentarily, his full attention shifted to Whip. "First of all, what the fuck—you thinking now? That's *my* job, so fall back. That shit becoming a bad habit." Clay mean mugged one of his right-hand men as the others, wide eyed, looked on. "And second—that's where *they* come in." He pointed at some of the youngsters that served as block captain lookouts. "I got two lawn mowers, saws, and a few shovels in the back of my truck." He tossed the keys to Dorie. "Go give each one of these workhorse fools a task and clean out two pathways on each end—one for coming and one for going."

"No disrespect, Clay," Dorie hesitantly spoke up before heading toward the door, "but that is a lot of work. It's gonna take some hours. Do you want these guys off post for that long? Who gonna watch for the police?"

"Fuck the police," Clay blurted out with contempt, pulling a thick knot from his front pocket. "Fuck 'em!" His pride and cockiness could be felt throughout the room. Having double-wrapped, beige-colored rubber bands barely holding the currency together, he grinned. "Now, you young PlayStation warriors trying to get paid or not? It's y'all call. Who want this bread?"

Without hesitation, five of the seven workers tripped over one another knowing if nothing else, at the end of the day, they'd be eating and smoking good thanks to Clay's generosity. The remaining two who were a little bit older and more seasoned in the dope game stood silent. After the overly eager five followed Dorie out the doorway, they cut into Clay about becoming new "alley crew leaders," which was fine with him. Promising them all bumps in salary if shit ran smoothly, everyone was happy—except for Whip who was still full of questions and doubt but was smart enough to keep it to himself.

Reverend Richards

"Bro, don't worry. I got you covered. I told you trust in the Lord."

"Bernard, kill all that God-will-provide bullshit you run on those people at your soup kitchen! Just spare me and tell me the plan."

"Well, there's one boy around here that's probably behind half, if not all, of the crime."

"Oh yeah?"

"Yeah, his name is Clay. And the thugs around this district damn near worship him."

"And?"

"And—as of last night, he and I became partners."

"Partners? Is *that* what you said?"

"Yes, partners," the reverend gleefully repeated. "He and I are throwing together to make a significant slow-down in crime in this district."

"And tell me this. Just how do a preacher and a dope dealer join forces like some Batman and Robin superhero motherfuckers to fight crime? You are messing around on a damn slippery slope."

"Easy. We both know some of the patrol cops from the Tenth Precinct are in my pocket and turn a blind eye when need be. Well, now they in Clay's too."

"What? What you saying?"

"I'm saying that young man has an unlimited freedom to sell as much drugs as he wants—no interference from me."

"Bernard—what in the hell!"

"I know it sounds crazy, but it's the only way to get those numbers down for you." Reverend Richards daydreamed. "Once you mayor and you appoint me to the citywide delegation, I can shut this God-forsaken program down and get me a new church and congregation. One with deeper pockets that like to give on Sunday mornings. After that, Clay and the rest of these low-life animals that live in this district can kill each other for all I care. I'm out."

"Damn, brother! I see carrying all those Bibles around ain't truly help you one bit." The power-driven candidate shook his head, holding his office phone close to his ear. "At the end of the day—you're the same person you used to be growing up . . . a conniving, manipulative, devious, jealous-hearted son of a bitch."

"Well, coming from you, the next mayor of Detroit," Reverend Richards chuckled, leaning back in his black leather chair, propping his feet up on the desk, "I'll take that as a compliment. Just know from now until the primary, me and that boy is gonna be tight . . . or so he gonna think we are."

"Bernard, you best be careful fooling around with that ruffian. Kids these days will kill you just as fast as they look at you."

"Don't worry," the reverend sat up, reaching for one of his many Bibles. "The deck is stacked, and I got God on my side."

***

The following days went by without incident. Whenever the police patrols rolled by, they turned a blind eye to Clay and his people. With the bushes and the paths cleared to and from the spot, they were getting served wide open. The crackheads seemed to like the setup much better as well. There was no confusion or line jumping. You'd get your product served like an assembly line and keep that shit moving.

Even though it had been less than seventy-two hours since the reverend and he had struck a deal of sorts, Clay noticed a spike in sales. Not having to temporary shut down when the lookouts spotted potential trouble headed in their direction, coupled with the fact his competition all of a sudden got hit hard by first the city narcos, then the Wayne County Sheriffs conducting raids, Clay did as he promised, sharing the additional revenue with the entire team.

No one questioned why he switched up the normal routine, and Clay didn't feel the need to offer an explanation, even to Whip and Dorie—his right-hand men. The front of the houses, the streets, and their residents were back to seemingly normal while the always-litter-filled alleys were off the chain. It was like stepping over from heaven to hell in a matter of seconds, depending on your pleasure. Reverend Richards had kept his end of the bargain, and Clay had done what he could in the way of putting a small Band-Aid on some of the crime. He and the preacher both knew trying to eliminate crime altogether in that hardheaded Detroit neighborhood was an impossible feat that even God himself couldn't pull off. Robbing, stealing, and killing were human instincts and the nature of the beast. And unfortunately for the law-abiding citizens like Mrs. Gale, Mr. and Mrs. Jessie, and countless others in the city—the beast was the only game in town.

Just as the good Reverend Richards used to make calls to fix things for his loyal and faithful parishioners—he was now making the calls on Clay's behalf.

Chapter Nineteen

Clay

"All right, Dorie, check this out. I want you and this crazy nigga here," Clay jokingly pointed to Whip, "to get here a little bit earlier and set up shop. We need to run wild with the rest of that hookup so we can make room for the new package."

"Oh yeah?" Dorie responded in a matter-of-fact way, brushing his waves.

"Yeah, dude. I'm gonna be kinda late. I gotsta swing by CVS and holler at old boy on that shit." Content on how things were going, he'd up'd the amount of dope he was copping. They were making money hand over fist the last few days and considering the ancient Chinese secret he was holding on to, he felt it was best to ride the rapids and come up while he could.

"Don't worry, boss," Whip bragged, grabbing at his nut sac, "I'm spending the night in the hood with this new bitch, so I'll be around here at the crack of dawn, for sure."

"Good, then I'll see both y'all in the a.m." Clay slid both his boys an extra $300, prepayment for the early-morning shift they were gonna put in, and pulled off heading home.

Reverend Richards

"Yeah, hello." The reverend almost knocked over the lamp on his nightstand as his phone rang.

"Yeah, hello, Bernard, it's me."

"Me who?" he groggily asked, rubbing the sleep out of the corners of his eyes.

"Your brother, that's who."

"What's wrong? What time is it?" Reverend Richards noticed it was still pitch black near the sides and top areas of his curtains. "What's going on?"

"You haven't watched the early-morning breaking news?"

"The news?" He immediately sat up searching for the remote. "No, I was asleep. What's on there? What channel?"

"Channel seven and two."

"Okay, let me see. It's just coming on."

"Well, apparently, one of these fool-ass teenagers was popping pills and jumped off the damn Belle Isle Bridge thinking he can fly."

"Oh yeah?" the preacher's television screen soon lit the otherwise dark room. "I see the Coast Guard now. But what's that got to do with me? And damn, bro, it's four-thirty in the morning!"

"Well, Bernard, while the Coast Guard was dragging the river searching for the body, they discovered some parts of a van."

"A van? Okay and—"

"And it is a city-owned van; a van belonging to the Water Department. The VIN numbers come back to the van those three missing workers were last spotted in. You know, in *your* district."

"Oh wow! Sweet baby Jesus!"

"Sweet baby Jesus, my ass. You know the bodies ain't far behind floating somewhere near the bottom! *Dateline, 20/20,* and my contacts at *CNN* all want a quote and a back-story to go with this bullshit! Man, I can see it now plastered on every national news organization. Detroit mayoral candidate and his brother throw a dragnet around crime in the very neighborhood those three innocent, hardworking city workers went missing in."

"That does sound good." Reverend Richards was all the way awake now, plotting with his kin.

"I know it does. And since you in cahoots with that drug dealer and know his method of operation, let's let him have it big time."

"Huh?" he puzzled, heading toward the bathroom. "What you mean?"

"I mean, by daybreak, the cameras and every reporter in town gonna be swarming all over the area those unlucky bastards were last spotted."

"And—"

"And why not give them bloodsucking media mongers something to report—something big—something major? Courtesy of me—the soon-to-be new mayor of Detroit."

"Yeah but—"

"Yeah but *nothing*, Bernard. You owe me, fool. Especially behind that last news conference you called on your damn own. Now get your head straight and to hell with that drug dealer. It was gonna be over for him sooner or later anyhow. So throw his criminal ass under the bus now. He ain't your family—I am."

"Is everybody in place?" Dorie asked as Whip bent the corner with a medium-size brown paper bag in tow. "Is them young hustlers ready to get this day started or what?"

Whip belched, throwing a small plastic red Faygo bottle into the bushes. "Yeah, them boys on post and the customers that gotsta punch that factory clock is already lined up; even that stuck-ass bitch in line waiting like she got some sense this morning!"

"Well, let's get this shit popping so we can start on the new rock 'em sock 'em Clay promised was next on deck." Dorie removed thirty-five safety pins which held twelve plastic dime baggie rocks of crack. "I'll get these to the fellas on the left side of the corner, and you can get the right, cool?"

"Yeah, we good, dawg." Whip took the bag back holding the remaining forty or so pins.

Getting their morning started, each posted up trying to sell out before Clay showed up.

Chapter Twenty

Clay

Climbing out of the bed, Clay stretched, standing in the mirror. Thinking he had to move soon since Rhonda's "keep-calling-good-bitter-ass" knew where he laid his head at, he frowned. *Never again. I swear on every dime I make, from now on out, I'm fucking these hoes at their room.* After taking a long, hot shower, Clay fell back on the bed with nothing but a towel wrapped around his waist. Daydreaming about how life was when he was a kid, he felt a cold, eerie chill in the air.

Fighting the overwhelming urge to stay in the house and just watch television all day, Clay got up and got dressed. Grabbing his cell, wallet, and keys, he was soon out the door. Still receiving a gang of anonymous calls to voice mail, he stopped by the nearest Metro PCS store getting them to change his phone number as soon as possible. Knowing he was running late to meet Ankit at the CVS for his bimonthly box of chemicals, he jumped down on the freeway. Next stop, the hood.

"Hey, now guy," Clay calmly greeted his foreign pharmaceutical connect leaning over the countertop. "You got me about ready?"

"No, Clay, no quite yet," he discreetly replied, not wanting his assistant to overhear his conversation. "I need some time to get some of these customers' prescriptions out the way; then I can get it together."

Looking over at the waiting area seats, Clay coincidently saw Mrs. Gale sitting down reading her Bible. "Hello."

"Well, hello, son, how are you?" She gave him a faint but reassuring smile. "Are you doing okay?"

"Yes, I'm okay. I'm just here taking care of some business." He looked back over his shoulder at the pharmacy. "Matter of fact, that fool ain't giving you any more problems, is he?"

"No, son, he is very respectful now. And thank you for that."

After getting her prescription, Clay asked Mrs. Gale to wait for him because he wanted to personally give her a ride home—this time, right to her front door. Of course, she obliged.

Chapter Twenty-one

Just like the preceding days, the block was running smooth. Everyone was getting served without arguing, complaining, or coming with shorts. Strangely, it seemed like the heads were even now getting trained to have their money out so they wouldn't slow down the progression of the next man getting high. It was like the addicts had formed a new union and code of ethics regarding the process.

"What's your count looking like, Dorie? How you holding?"

"Man, Whip, we clocking on my side. These young boys ain't playing around with they ass. We making that bread."

"My side neither. We cranking. You know, I'm putting my foot on they throat to push this shit pronto." Whip pulled out his cell pushing Clay's number. "Matter of fact, let me call this nigga and see if he want us to run an 'early-morning blast' special on this last shit we holding."

"Yeah, do that," Dorie quickly agreed, counting the ticket money out in the open.

"Man, what the fuck?"

"What's good, nigga? What's the deal?" He continued his count glancing up.

"Naw, Dorie, hold up. Maybe I'm bugging." Whip pushed Clay's contact number and was once again met with an annoying disconnection recording. "How in the fuck this wannabe hood rich motherfucker gonna have his phone turned off? Damn!"

Before Dorie could respond to Whip's sarcastic rant, all hell broke loose, catching everyone—the workers, drug addicts, and neighbors alike—completely off guard. From every direction possible—north, south, east, and west—swarms of the Detroit Police Department strategically invaded Clay's stronghold-controlled environment in full force. Obviously having every single detail suited and out on the street, crime in other parts of the cash-strapped city had to be catapulting.

The Gang Squad chased down worker after worker through the thick, unsafe pathways that only the teens knew. With money flying and drugs being thrown, some "should-be track stars" ultimately got caught; others safely got away. The narcotics officers and the uniformed patrol cops tried their best corralling the multitudes of scattering customers in one sweep, but that didn't work out as planned. Once again, the people who rip and ran the streets, walked the streets, lived in the streets, and used drugs in the streets, knew all the shortcuts and emergency escape routes, leaving the cops coming up short. Most, if not all, of the officers had families to go home to and weren't interested in being dead heroes trying to venture into the unknown world these dealers and disease-infested junkies called home. So whoever they could easily catch, good. The others, so be it. They'd have to see them at a later date.

Reverend Richards

Keeping an eye out for Clay, he felt some sort of way for double crossing him so quickly. With the news cameras from every station in the city and some national ones rolling, a still gleeful and proud Reverend Richards grinned. With his chest stuck out, he stood shoulder to shoulder alongside his mayoral candidate brother. As his sibling made a long-winded speech detailing him and his "loyal to restoring the neighborhood to peace" plan to capture these deviants and return to the true tranquility that should be within the city of Detroit boundaries, Reverend Richards gloated. With a backdrop of young, angry, handcuffed thugs and zoned-out-faced addicts being roughly escorted to awaiting police vehicles, the brothers took the opportunity to shine and, hopefully, garnish votes from the current administration.

"Believe me when I tell you all this . . . Now I'm not saying the mayor has not been doing his job; it's hard in a crime-infested city like this to stop illegal activities. But a blatant out-in-the-open organized drug transaction for the entire world to see is—and should be—totally unacceptable. If this was going on in the suburbs, it wouldn't fly—so why in Detroit? Why here? The people deserve better. If I were mayor, we'd be kicking down doors of criminals, even the so-called residents that oftentimes aid the dealers in exchange for money. People should not condone, facilitate, or tolerate this type of activity." His carefully worded speech went on as Dorie and Whip were finally apprehended and led out of the rear of an abandoned house. *"Now the reign of terror on this neighborhood is temporarily shut down, and as my brother, Reverend Bernard Richards, can testify to, this day has been a long time coming. From selling drugs, stolen Walmart trucks, dead bodies discarded, and, of course, those poor Water Department workers last seen alive in this district, under my new leadership, if elected, things will most certainly change. If you don't believe me—look behind me. This day was successful because with the assistance of the police, my brother's detailed information about the drug dealers, and the help of dedicated citizens, we can make this city great again! Thank you!"*

Clay

"I'm glad that fool back in there has been acting like he has good sense." Clay helped the elderly woman up into his truck. "I would hate to have to speak to him again."

"No, son, I told you it's okay. It really is."

"Well, that's all that matters. He should've known his place." Clay made sure the radio was turned off before starting the engine. "Sit back, and I'll have you home in no time."

While they were riding, Mrs. Gale held her Bible tightly, finding the courage to ask the young dope dealer a personal question. "Clay, where is your family, son? Your mother, father, brothers, sisters?"

After a brief silence, Clay finally spoke. "Well, to be honest with you, I don't have a family. I'm out here alone and have been since I was way younger."

"Oh no, son. My goodness, no," Mrs. Gale grandmotherly sympathized. "By yourself?"

"Yeah," he kinda smiled while nodding. "I been homeless, broke, hungry, in and out of juvenile and jail my whole life. Don't nobody care about me but me."

"That's terrible, son. Whatever happened to at least your mother, if you don't mind me asking?"

"My mother?" Clay replied with a faint sigh. "She died when I was younger. She was dealing with a lot of issues; kinda like depression. And as for my father, I don't even know who he is. I never did. My mother acted like it was some type of top secret lie, and she took the truth to the grave with her. So like I said, I been out here on my own. I still am. For real for real, no one cares about me or if I live or die. I'm just another nigga out here trying to eat day to day. But I'm good with that. That's life!"

"Don't say that, son. God loves you if no one else does."

"Well, if that was true, then, dawg, I mean, God has a strange way of showing it."

"Well, when in doubt, son, pray. He'll answer you. Trust me, he will. God will show up and show out when you least expect him to!"

Clay never knew God to show for him, but he didn't have the heart to dispute the old woman. As they pulled up on the block, Clay could immediately see something was wrong. The quietness in the air was strange, to say the least. The entire block appeared deserted of all the familiar faces he had on his payroll. Besides some of the whispering neighbors, Mr. and Mrs. Jessie, and Trinity pushing her kids in a stroller, the street seemed to be two seconds away from tumbleweeds blowing by. Even Mrs. Gale knew something just wasn't right. There were no teenagers darting in between the fields, no crackheads walking down the sidewalk like zombies, and no cars lined up near the alleyway.

"What in the hell?" Clay snatched his cell off the console dialing first Dorie's number, then Whip's. Weirdly, each call went straight to voice mail. "Damn! What the fuck?"

As Mrs. Gale got out of the truck on her own, she was soon met by Mr. and Mrs. Jessie, who looked worried. Trinity, wide eyed, wasted no time pushing the stroller in the middle of the street and up to Clay's driver-side window.

"Clay, I'm glad you wasn't here. It was crazy."

"What was fucking crazy, girl? What the fuck happened around this motherfucker? What the fuck!"

"This morning, out of nowhere, the ho-ass police showed up."

"What?"

"Yeah, they came from every-damn-where. It was like some shit off of TV." She waved her hands around explaining what she'd seen and heard. "One minute, people was getting served back around there," she pointed toward the alley. "Then, *bam,* here come sirens and cars from every direction. A fucking helicopter was even flying overhead."

"You bullshitting." Clay kept his foot on the gas. "What about Dorie and Whip? You seen them?"

"Yeah, after they caught some of the runners and some heads, they finally caught them."

"Aww, fuck, naw!"

"Yeah, it was all on the news. That fucked-up, creepy-ass Reverend Richards and his brother was all in front of the cameras talking that shit."

"The reverend?"

"Yeah, and they was mentioning," she got closer to the truck so no one could hear their conversation, "they found that van those ho-ass niggas was driving."

"What ho-ass niggas? What you talking about?" Clay frowned as his eyes scanned the block focusing on the Outreach Building.

"Them guys that tried to . . . you know," she lowered her head in shame. "It's all over the news."

"Fuck." Clay slammed his fist on the side of the steering wheel, causing Trinity and her kids to jump.

"Listen, if you want to, you can drive down to my house and see it on television," she suggested. "They been playing that bullshit footage all damn day."

"Yeah, all right. I'll meet you down there," Clay agreed just as Rhonda's good-stalking ass slowly drove by mean mugging both he and Trinity.

When Clay finally finished watching the informative news interview, he was livid. He was more pissed than he'd been in years. It was bad enough his entire crew, including Whip and Dorie, were locked up, and he had lost thousands of dollars in revenue and was in line to spend more on bail for them, but at this point, he could give a fuck less if the Coast Guard discovered the van or the three bodies, even though Trinity volunteered to go to the police and tell them what the shady trio had tried to do to her. None of that mattered to him. He could and would deal with whatever. That was part of the game and the bullshit that came with the territory.

However, Reverend Bernard Richards and the backstabbing betrayal that rat bastard had obviously orchestrated was another. Clay didn't deal well with one man pissing on another just the fuck because he could. That was a serious no-no. There was some rules to the game, and the reverend had violated Clay's code of ethics. His name was his name in the streets of Detroit, and hiding behind the cloth of Jesus himself wasn't gonna stop Clay from revenge. That was the point, and the principle consequences be damned.

After he contacted his lawyer to start bailing his people out that couldn't get released on personals, Clay jumped back in his truck driving off to gather his thoughts.

Chapter Twenty-two

Retribution

Reverend Richards was beyond feeling himself. Although he hadn't actually talked to Clay personally, he knew his team was locked up and the block was quiet. There were hardly any users in search of drugs, no teenagers on the corners looking out for the cops, and no one harassing and begging folk for spare change. Having called the Block Club president several times since the impromptu raid trying to hear if he'd seen Clay and not receiving an answer, Reverend Richards decided to go and knock on Mr. Jessie's front door. He knew even if Mrs. Gale had heard from Clay, she probably wouldn't tell him, especially since their last controversial conversation.

Knowing Clay didn't and wouldn't have the nerve to show up on the hot, high-profile street, the cocky preacher started his slow stroll victory walk up the block. Waiting for the well dressed schoolteacher to drive by he'd threatened with exposure if she didn't stay away, he laughed, knowing she couldn't purchase her drugs today—not in his neighborhood. Passing the two Muslim kids going to the store for their mother, he forced them to speak, even though they didn't want to. Getting closer to Mr. and Mrs. Jessie who were in their yard talking to Mrs. Gale, the reverend got his game face on.

"Hello, neighbors," he greeted them.

"Hello." The group response was cold.

"I'm glad all of you good people are out here," he gloated in a condescending manner. "That way, it'll make it easier for y'all to thank me for doing what y'all didn't have the courage to do all these years."

"What?" Mrs. Jessie spoke out in an angry tone.

"Yeah, what, motherfucker?" Clay eased through a vacant lot gun in hand with Trinity trailing behind. "Tell us all why we should be thankful to you again."

"Clay!" Reverend Richards was shocked as were the rest of them.

"Yeah, nigga. It's me—what you thought? Me and you got unfinished business."

"Say what now—unfinished business?" Mrs. Jessie wasn't done trying to get an understanding as the school-teacher now parked, walked around the corner, blending in with the others.

"Yeah, this snake nigga was supposed to be calling my black ass when and if the cops were coming. Instead, he flipped the script. Threw a nigga right under the bus and drove that motherfucker himself, didn't you?"

"Naw, Clay! I didn't! I wouldn't do that!"

"Come on now, Rev, have some pride about yourself. Be a man about yours like you wanted me to be so damn bad. Boss the fuck up just one time, old man—one freaking time."

"Wait! Wait! Come on now, please, wait! This is a mistake; nothing but a huge misunderstanding between two men. This ain't right, son; it ain't." Easily, you could hear the sound of sheer uncut desperation drag out in each syllable of each word. Praying to God he was any-where else other than where he was at this very moment, he defensively held up his hands. Taking several deep breaths, he felt his chest heave in and out. It was hard to speak, all things considered, but the reverend pushed through. "Do you know what you doing? You can't, you just can't," he shouted answering his own question.

"Say what? Are you serious, old conniving house nigga?" The reply came swiftly, knowing time was ticking by and the police might show up at any given moment.

"Are you high on something? Wait; put that gun down. Put it down. Please." Once more, the overly desperate words rang throughout the entire city block. "Remember, 'vengeance is mine sayeth the Lord.' You need to think about what you're proposing to do, son. This ain't God's way."

"You funny as shit right about now, but it ain't gonna work out for you, playa. Not this time, not today. You official fucked in the game."

"No no no! Hold up! This ain't right," the preacher's bargaining to live to conduct another Sunday service continued. His mouth kept moving, but the words coming out were obviously redundant and falling upon deaf ears.

"Shut the fuck up." The tension grew as the jaws of several people standing around dropped wide open. "Matter of fact, Rev, shut the fuck up before I shut you all the way up. See I'm a real nigga 24/7 with mines. I don't talk shit and strong-arm motherfuckers. I say what I mean and mean what the fuck I say. So stop begging and negotiating; you done."

There was nothing but tears on both cheeks. With warm stinging piss running down his creased pants leg, Reverend Richards waved his tattered, covered Bible wildly in the air. At this point, he would do and say just about anything to escape his punishment. He showed absolutely no pride. Time for all of that was over. Praying his words would work and the hardened criminal, sea-soned thug would show him a small bit of mercy, the reverend continued. "Look, you gotta listen to what I'm saying. Please, I don't deserve this. I'm begging you. It was all just a misunderstanding; a big damn mistake."

"You don't deserve this, huh? Yeah, right. Come on, now, Rev—don't play yourself and don't be standing out in these grimy Detroit streets acting innocent. Begging is out of season around these parts. Correct my black ass if a nigga wrong, but I warned you not to jump out there with me. I done told you I'm one of them motherfuckers that make fools act right whether they want to or not."

"Please, Clay, please. This ain't God's way," the terrified man continued to plead hoping, for a Hail Mary miracle. "Let *him* handle my final judgment. He has the final say."

"God's way—old man, please. I got the final say today; trust that. And would you stop pretending like you give a damn about me and my fucking soul? Keep it a hundred, with your money-hungry ass." Clay's clean-shaven bald head sweated in the scorching hot summer sun. As his blue jean shorts slightly sagged, showing the upper band of his boxers, his unlaced Tims stayed firmly planted on the curb. Tightly, he held the rubber grip handle of the gun. Strange as it may be, it seemed to be eagerly urging Clay to hurry the hell up and kill the lying son of a bitch standing in front of him taking a cop. "Rev . . . You know you ain't about nothing. And all these weak-minded cowards out here looking at me like I'm half crazy after you done blackmailed them should know the bullshit too. Man of the cloth—yeah, right; you straight foul. I'm surprised somebody ain't been bodied your punk ass."

"Don't do it, son. He ain't worth the bullet," a random voice nonsympathetically shouted from the small group of spell struck spectators. "He'll answer for his sins one day."

"Listen, if you or anybody else don't wanna see this nickel slick Negro pay for what he done did, then I suggest y'all go home—'cause today is his fucking day," he responded after hawking a huge glob of spit in his soon-to-be victim's face. Clay wasn't in the mood for any interference of what he planned on doing. He was 100 percent official with his. Raised in the streets, he couldn't be easily manipulated. He wouldn't be conned by "the Word," like so many others, in the uncompassionate crowd the preacher had "worked his magic on" in the past, had been. The blank, dark expression in the youngster's stare told it all. It revealed he could care less about the many potential eyewitnesses that stood idly by. If he caught a murder case, then so be it. It was what it was. Clay was intent on revenge, and today was that day.

Reverend Richards, dry throat, struggled to speak. Short of breath, he grew nauseated. He was sick to his stomach. Panic-stricken, his breakfast and lunch wasted no time reappearing. Gagging from the smell and sight of his own vomit, his heart rate increased. Realizing the local dope boy wasn't trying to hear one of his long drawn out sermons, he hyperventilated. He knew the end was drawing near as the tears flowed from his eyes and snot slid down his jaw. Life in Detroit had never been more real in his fifty-one years of living than it was at this moment. He had never been so terrified. He had never been so regretful of his actions. He wanted to repent for everything wrong he had done or said over the past few decades but knew it was way too much for God to forgive. He wanted to believe a miracle was seconds away, but it had yet to come.

"Son, just listen to me. You gotta listen. Hear me out," Reverend Richards, with hands folded, begged in vain, stalling the inevitable. *Where are the authorities when you need them? What's taking them so long? Why haven't none of these people called the police? God, please help me! Please stop this savage from what he has planned. I know I've been doing wrong and not honoring your Word, but please, Lord. Please save me from this boy's wrath. I can change. Just let help come.* Desperate, he wondered when, and if, the police would show up in time to save his life. "I can switch things up. I can clear up all the confusion that has you so angry. I'm serious. Clay, just let me make a call to my people. Let me call my brother. It was just a huge misunderstanding. I swear," he loudly alleged, begging for his life. "Please, for God's sake—one call."

That was it. It was over, and Clay had heard enough. No more time-outs; no more reprieves; and no more lies of making right all the wrongs he'd done. Fed up with hearing the man beg, Clay let one round off. His aim was dead-on. Striking the so-called man of the cloth directly in the left kneecap, stunned neighbors covered their ears to deaden the sound. The good reverend dropped his Bible. From that point on, it was as if everything were moving in slow motion. In agony, not able to stand, the constantly scheming preacher collapsed onto the pavement. His head just missed slamming into the edge of the litter-filled curb. With an immediate gush of dark-colored blood quickly leaking through Reverend Richards's dress pants, one elderly woman looked away while strangely, another person wickedly smirked with satisfaction.

Slowly walking up on the now-sobbing pastor, Clay didn't smile. He didn't frown or show any real true sentiment about what he'd just done or was about to do. This was a part of street life to him; revenge on his enemy when need be. Towering over the cowardly older man, Clay finally sneered with contempt. With his gun still held tightly in one hand, he made use of the other. Ruthlessly, he snatched the gold chain and diamond cross from the wounded man's neck, letting it fall to the ground. Clay was hell-bent on what had to come next. *God can't save your ass this time. You done fucked over way too many motherfuckers.* Still showing no emotion or regret, Clay coldly placed the muzzle of his pistol to the trembling, corrupt preacher's wrinkled forehead. As the small crowd of neighbors watched in disbelief . . . but oddly content, Clay taunted his moaning prey one final time.

"You fake hypocrite—you predator. One call. Is that all you need, one more call? Your credibility is like below zero with me," Clay, standing over the man, vengefully mocked his victim, still showing no mercy. His winter-white wife beater showed off every angry, bulging muscle and every ink-carved tattoo. Lifting his right boot, Clay slammed the sole directly into the middle of the older man's chest. "Your days of 'making calls' and 'fixing thangs' around the way are over. Negotiations are over—believe that. You gotsta give another pint or two for all your sins. How about that for God's so-called homeboy?"

"But no—no; wait, wait," the unscrupulous preacher raised one hand upward. In excruciating pain, the other clutched his bloodied, bone-shattered knee. His eyes desperately searched the onlookers he knew so well for compassion but found none. "Don't y'all see this?" he belted out with tears flowing and his voice cracking. "After all the things I've done for each of you—why isn't anybody stopping him?" His weakening tone vibrated with every syllable that passed across his quivering lips. "Oh my God, one of y'all, please, call the police before he shoots me again! I'm begging in Jesus Christ's name, help me."

Reverend Bernard Richards, the head director of West Side Outreach Ministries, lay bleeding to death in the middle of the pothole-filled Detroit street. Residents

were stunned but not budging from where they were.
Instead, they stood around whispering. Yet strangely, no
one bothered to call for help as their once-beloved minister had asked. Not sanctified senior citizen Thelma Gale,
who lived in the apartment building on the crime-ridden
block. Not nosy Mr. Jessie, the Block Club president,
who wanted things to go back to the days of the past. Not
Mr. Jessie's constantly depressed wife called for help.
Troubled, drug-addicted teacher, Lynn Banks, teenager
Abdul and his little sister all had the opportunity to dial
911 on their cells. Hard as it was to believe, they chose
not to. Trinity, a young single mother, nonchalantly
cleaned underneath her fingernails while she recorded
the altercation soon-to-turn-murder on her Android. It
was as if the group was merely watching a movie rather
than being firsthand witnesses to a cold-blooded murder
about to take place. Nevertheless, none of the preacher's
seemingly loyal parishioners who he "supposedly helped"
shed a single tear. He was on his own and had to face the
music by himself. God was about to call him home . . . or
the devil one. Either way it went, Clay was gonna end his
life.

"Look at you . . . the-all-so-great-and-above-the-laws-
of-the-hood Reverend Richards. Out here begging the
next dude and the neighborhood people for mercy that
you shit over on the regular. Imagine that; you acting like
a real pussy right about now. A real little bitch around
these parts," Clay grinned, finally feeling a true sense
of accomplishment as he went on. "You need to man up
'cause you can't do jack for me or with me no more. That's
history."

"No . . . Wait, Clay."

"No, *you* wait. Truth is, playtime is over, fool. You
earned each one of these hot motherfuckers you about
to get. Time for you to go all the way to damn sleep. I'm
tight on you."

"Please, Clay." In denial, the man's eyes grew wider while still holding on to hope, holding on to the notion his wrongdoing was bigger than the game itself.

"Tell the devil I'll see him later. Now, bleed out, bitch nigga." Clay happily let loose another deadly deliberate round.

Squad car sirens were finally blaring in the far distance answering a mysterious "shots fired" call. All the seemingly innocent bystanders scattered, disappearing into their homes. No one wanted to risk getting questioned by the law. No one wanted to get judged for not being the one who had not called the authorities. There was a motionless body outside of their dwellings. It was sprawled in the middle of the street on display, leaking blood from the gaping bullet holes. Peeking out from behind their curtains and front doors, no one truly cared as the county coroner lastly arrived on the scene. Officially pronouncing the good Reverend Richards dead in the middle of the street, his now sheet-covered body was removed. As far as the neighborhood witnesses were concerned, the reverend was just another casualty; another statistic in Detroit's ever-rising homicide rate. However, to the Detroit Police Department, he was the front-runner-to-be-elected mayor's half brother and top priority on the long list of murders to solve. Discovering the true, raw, uncut circumstances that led to a supposedly godly man being laid out in the middle of an open-air, drug-infested street in broad daylight is where they had to start.

Chapter Twenty-three

The Manhunt

There was no question what was going on in District 5 as well as the entire city. The streets were running red in Detroit. With constant meetings with various officials, there were still no solutions in clear sight. For the time being, it was what it was. The criminals did what they wanted to, and the cops did what they could. It was a dangerous game of cat and mouse for all parties involved. If things were not and had not been bad enough, now the authorities were dealt yet another bad hand. They had to solve this case of what appeared to be premeditated, cold-blooded murder quickly. The mayor and police chief warned that the feds were only a few dead bodies away from stepping in and taking over. The homicide detectives investigating the multiple murders, including Reverend Richards's, had no choice but to up their game. They had already asked for the surveillance cameras from the church building which were, of course, handed over. Unfortunately, they were not in the proper position to see much of anything useful. They then had to forcefully subpoena the tapes from the liquor store; yet, as fate would have it, the cameras facing the rear of the store and block were broken. Seemingly hundreds of tips came in to the hotline number that was set up exclusively for murder tips. Each and every one had to be checked out. The officers didn't want to run the risk of ignoring any possible leads. Doing so may have resulted in allowing a killer to roam free longer than need be. Day and night, night and day, the lines were answered. After several dead ends, the detectives finally got a call that had a strong possibility of panning out. The caller seemed to know what they were talking about but refused to leave any contact information. That small bone was thrown to the cops, giving them hope but didn't last. They were back where they started, at square one. Sitting around discussing what new jobs they could try to find after surely being fired from their present ones, the tension in the air was serious. With the clock ticking, any hopes of capturing the preacher's killer grew dim.

Clay

Reverend Richards's homicide was not easily solved in forty-eight hours. A considerable amount of time elapsed. Residents were terrified there was a brutal, coldhearted killer on the loose. Yet, each of the seven neighbors who had stood mute watching him murdered continued to keep their mouths shut. For their own individual reasons, they ignored what they'd witnessed. As strange as it may seemed to persons who were white and lived much different lifestyles, the residents were carrying on with their everyday lives. Whether it was the fact they were being loyal to the local drug dealer or had contempt for the preacher's recent choices, they chose silence.

However, the crime-solving gods were finally on the detectives' side. Thanks to an out-of-the-blue anonymous tip, a suspect was named in the high-profile, street-justice-style execution. Breaking news on every television channel, the cops were gearing up as if they were in pursuit of the devil himself after escaping from hell. First, they kicked in the door of Clay's apartment, then both the spot and the hookup house again. His picture was plastered on every channel and every avenue of social media. People were warned that he was considered to be armed and extremely dangerous. Anyone caught assisting in his avoiding arrest would be charged with obstructing justice and contempt of the law. Hours dragged by. Thankfully, the long, exhausting police manhunt hours finally paid off. Clay Jennings, who had no family to speak of or true friends to count on, was apprehended. Handcuffed and shackled on his ankles, he was roughly thrown in the rear of a squad car. Paraded before the reporters, he was read his rights as he gave them a look of defiance. The often-feared infamous narcotic dealer was soon booked and fingerprinted at police headquarters. The charge was suspicion of first-degree murder.

Stripped of the suede laces from his Tims and the Gucci belt that barely held up his sagging jeans, he held his head high. The suspected cold-blooded killer was not moved. "You think y'all doing something so fucking big? You think y'all got a nigga like me buffaloed? Well, you don't. I'm a boss through and through, so it's whatever." Clay was not shaken one bit when the detectives mocked that he would be going to jail for the rest of his life. "It ain't no way in hell I'm going to jail for some bogus shit y'all trying to put on me. Y'all some frauds. I don't even know why y'all had my picture and shit all over the news like I'm Capone or Bin Laden." Strong in his pride, Clay failed to blink when the detectives claimed they had the murder weapon and his prints were all over it. He knew they were bluffing then for sure, because he had dismantled the pistol and tossed the various parts here and there into the murky Detroit River. "Man, y'all need to quit bullshitting and get the fuck outta here. Them mind games ain't gonna work on me. If y'all got a gun I used to do any dumb shit, then by all means, please produce that motherfucker! Please do!"

Staring the suit-and-tie men coldly in the eye, Clay proceeded to smirk when told that they had several witnesses who were more than willing to testify. Although he knew this was the only thing the cops were probably being honest about, he still kept it gangster. He could care less and refused to let them see him sweat. From his point of view, he did what he had to do, and definitely what had to be done. It was the principle of it all. If Clay allowed the crooked man of the cloth to do all the ungodly things he had done and not call him to task, he couldn't rule the streets as he had been doing. "Yeah, hurry the hell up and lock up my black ass. Then do what y'all do. And remember, I know what damn time it is. Y'all gonna have to show any proof real quick."

In handcuffs, the crazed, ruthless assailant was led to an empty holding cell on the ninth floor by the lead detective. "Trust me, it's nothing. I'm a different breed than most, believe that. Get the fuck on and go do y'alls damn job." Spitting on the concrete floor, a huge glob of saliva barely missed the man's polished shoes. As the officer stepped back, he slammed the bars shut. Clay showed no real remorse. He looked around at his new short-term surroundings and took a deep breath before exhaling. As he fell back onto the bottom metal bunk, he thought to himself that things had to go down exactly as they did.

You could almost hear the electricity in the stale, mildew air. Clay reflected back to the last month or so and what ultimately got him where he was now; locked up with seemingly no chance whatsoever of beating the case. His demons were the only thing he had to keep him company; and that they did. Clay was used to them taking over his mind, in good times and definitely now, in bad. Unlike the other major Ls he'd taken throughout the years, Clay wasn't too sure he'd bounce back from this setback.

Fuck that snake. The reverend ain't know who in the hell he was dealing with this time. They lucky I ain't put something hot in his head earlier. That dirty rat-ass bastard had it coming. I wish I could kill him all over again. Now, these weak-ass police wanna try to hem a brother up. I know a dude like me gonna get the book thrown at me this go-around. I know one, if not all, of them professional victims out there gonna testify against my black ass. Shitttt, but I ain't going out like this! They trying to have me fucked up in the brain like my momma was when she left this earth, but it ain't gonna work. Clay reflected back, and his memories of his mother were nothing good.

"Damn, I ain't trying to be funny or no slick shit like that," Clay frowned, tired of all the mind games his mother had started playing over the past few years.

"Baby, what are you talking about? Come sit down and talk to your momma. She wanna read you something, something that's gonna make you get right with the Lord."

"Say what, now? Excuse the hell outta me, but since when did you start giving a fuck about me and my well-being, huh, Ma?"

"Baby, I always have cared about you. You're the only thing that matters to me." She clutched a Bible she'd no doubt stolen out of a motel room she'd been in with some trick-ass nigga.

"You know we ain't even like that with each other now, don't you? When a nigga was little and crying every night for you to stay home and 'care about me,' you was

out somewhere ghost. So now I'm out here doing me."
Rolling his eyes with intensity, everything about this
out-of-the-blue conversation was starting to aggravate
the young street warrior in the worst type of way
known to mankind.

"Clay, enough is enough! You really need to let go of
the past, baby; please. If you haven't noticed from all
your destructive behavior, look around. It's practically
eating you alive. And if you keep skipping school and
getting caught stealing, they gonna lock you up."

"Like you really give a shit. I'm the only one that cares
about me. And guess what? When you go off into your
little crazy acts, I'm out here getting money for us to pay
bills and eat. So fuck what you talking about. Matter of
fact, go sit down somewhere and take your medication."

"Clay, I've been telling you for years now, I'm a
changed person. For God's sake, can't you see that? I'm
not that woman anymore!"

"What in the entire fuck! Damn, Ma, shut that shit up
and stop trying to drive me crazy like your ass. For once,
try to keep it real with me and get off your soapbox. It's
not enough days in the week or weeks in the years to
undo who and what you are now. So you can do me a
favor and fall all the way back with that get-over-it-
and-move-on routine you running. Trust when I tell
you, I'm straight on all that. Even who my father really
is; I'm straight on that shit too. Save your sob story of
redemption for the Lord you all of sudden love so damn
much more than them random dudes you been laying
up with since I was little. It was bad enough I had to
stick 'Uncle James's ass way back when, but you still
kept bugging."

"Clay, stop it," she begged with tears in her eyes,
knowing full well her son was telling the truth.

"I will, no problem. Ain't no thang. I've gotta go any-how. I got real shit to do with real motherfuckers that's out here in these streets making money." In his eyes, flat-out, his mother would always be that over-the-top, crazy, pill-popping tramp that he learned his addictive behavior from. *As far as Clay was concerned, for that reason—amongst a thousand or so countless other ones the bad seed could easily name—she wasn't about to get treated with nothing more than a swift fuck-you long and hard and good-the-hell-bye.*

It would be days, sometimes weeks, before Clay would show back up at the house. And when he did, there was always drama. Soon, he'd had enough of her erratic mental behavior and stayed gone for good. It had been several months when he had run into one of his old neighbors. Tragically, they informed him that his once-beloved mother had taken too many pills, ran out of the house half-crazed, and darted into oncoming traffic. Her frail body was not strong enough to endure the force of the SUV accidentally running her down. When Clay found that news out, he vowed from that day forward he would never be down and out. He'd always stay on top of his game and never *ever* allow the next person to drive him crazy like his moms. He would be the controller of his own destiny.

As Clay was having a not-so-good trip down memory lane going on, one by one, the seven reported witnesses to the good Reverend Bernard Richards's demise were being rounded up for questioning. Clay Jennings was a citywide known infamous drug lord. He was a street enforcer, extortionist, and repeat offender of almost every law on the books. As far as the Detroit Police

Homicide Division was concerned, this blatant, broad daylight murder case would be open and shut. However, things were never as they seemed in the city they were paid peanuts to serve and protect. They would soon be fighting against the odds they had felt were easily in their favor.

Chapter Twenty-four

The Cops

Now that the police had their suspect behind bars on suspicion of murder, they had to make the charge stick. Not only had the anonymous caller given them the name of Reverend Richards's killer, but the names of some supposed eyewitnesses to the deadly feat. After checking each name out, the detectives were jointly baffled as to why they had failed to speak out. By all accounts, each was a law-abiding citizen. The only reason that could be cited for their silence was fear of retaliation and threats from Clay's cohorts who remained lurking the streets. Wanting to close out this case and move on to the next, the sure-to-be-an-exhausting day was already planned out for the detectives. One by one, the seven reported witnesses to the demise of the good Reverend Bernard Richards, the soon-to-be mayor's half brother, were brought in for questioning. Clay Jennings was a known drug lord, street enforcer, extortionist, and repeat offender of almost every law on the books. As far as the Detroit Police Homicide Division was concerned, this blatant broad daylight murder case would soon be open and shut.

The first one to get interviewed was Lynn Banks. The detectives thought that there must have been some sort of a mistake when her name came up. Her plate number was supposedly written down, saying her vehicle was parked on the corner the day of the murder. She was rumored to be outside of the car and on the block. With no criminal record to speak of, the detectives wanted to question why someone of her background was even on the drug-infested block in the first place.

"So, Ms. Banks, let me get this right. I'm kinda confused and definitely need some clarity. You were in the general vicinity of the murder that day, correct? And you saying you didn't see or hear anything out of the ordinary at all, is that true?" the detective skeptically inquired, trying to read her body movements and gestures. "You didn't hear anything—no gunshots, no people screaming or maybe running away? Come on now, think about it hard."

Lynn Banks did think back to that very day in question, and also the days that led up to it. She got a chill as she thought about the reverend threatening to inform the school board about her drug use. Truly addicted, she knew they would've listened to a man of his standing and had her tested—most certainly ending her career. Ms. Banks was far from a fool. The multiple-having-degree educator wanted no part of any police investigation, let alone a murder case. With a straight face, she decided it would be in her best interest to keep her mouth shut. She'd just pretend she was trying to locate the home of one of her students. Not to mention, Clay had asked her on more than one occasion why was she lowering her standards smoking crack. Through all her multiple times on the block copping, she felt some sort of way that a dope dealer saw more good in her that she had in herself over the past few years. That made her see Clay in a much different light and hold him in a higher regard. Taking all of that into consideration, she spoke out again. "I'm so very sorry I can't help you gentlemen. I saw the news report, and I think it's horrible—just terrible. But like I said, it's true, indeed, that I was in that general vicinity. But I was preoccupied on my cell trying to locate an address."

"And what address was that again?" the man quizzed, trying to trip her up.

"I already told you earlier I wrote the name of the street down wrong and was confused and lost. That's why I was on my cell trying to call the school office."

"Oh yeah, you did say that. Well, thank you for coming in. And once again, our apologies we had to send an officer to your house, and then classroom, but we only had your license plate number to go off of, and this is an extremely serious case. We may need to ask you a few more questions, but for now, that's it."

After escorting her to the elevator, the detectives sat down at their desks. Going over the notes they separately took as Lynn Banks explained being in that crime-ridden neighborhood, each felt there was something off about her story, yet they couldn't quite put their finger on it. Hopefully, one of the others slated to come in could shed more light on Reverend Richards's death.

With fingers crossed this next interview would go better than the first, they could only wait. The next people to be questioned pertaining to what they may have witnessed arrived a few minutes before they were due. The detectives took that as a positive sign—that was . . . until the elevator door opened. There stood two children who were accompanied by their stern-faced Muslim father. With one foot barely outside of the elevator, he started on a verbal tirade. He was not only offended by having to be there, but the means it took to do so.

"Look, I don't know why you are harassing my children. Going to their school and arousing unwarranted suspicion as if they are some sort of criminals! Why is it that you sent the police to my front door? I don't appreciate it one bit. Why are we being targeted? Why are my children being disrespected? Is it because we are Muslim? Is *that* why?" His long beard and green leather-covered Quran seemed to take over the small room. He stood proud as his rant grew more militant in defense of his and his children's civil liberties being tested. "We have civil rights, and they won't be violated. We are all American citizens. I was born here. They were born here. It's bad enough my kids get bullied almost every day at school, but do you supposed officers of the law do anything to prevent *that?* Do something about *that* travesty, then I can support you."

Charged with the duty to serve and protect, the detectives were dumbfounded. They certainly did not expect this type of reaction when told the witnesses had arrived. Thrown off, each had to quickly readjust to how they handled the children as well as their dad.

"Hello. I'm sorry about that, and no, sir, it's not like that at all. To me personally, I don't care what religion you are; we are all the same." The detective was careful of the words he was using, knowing he wanted to avoid any allegations of racial profiling. "It's just that a reliable source puts both your children on the scene of the murder of Reverend Richards. And seeing how they are potential witnesses, we have no choice but to investigate, religion and citizenship aside. The only thing we want to know is what the two of them may have seen that day."

"I understand that; however, for you to send several police cars to show up at my front door—sirens and lights flashing—*that* I have a problem with; a *very serious* problem. You treated my children as if they were the murderer of that man instead of innocent witnesses."

The other detective knew the father was correct. He knew they were being overzealous in an attempt to bring this high-profile case to a close. He had ordered all the assumed witnesses notified of the circumstances and put on notice to come in as soon as possible or risk being arrested.

"Sir, once again, the department as a whole, and I, myself, personally, do apologize. We just want to ask your children a few questions about the day Reverend Richards was murdered, if we may; then we will let you leave."

"*Excuse* me. *Let us leave?* We did nothing wrong for you to *let* us do *anything!* Should I get a lawyer? If so, be advised we will say nothing more until our legal representative arrives."

"No, no—sorry. I didn't mean it like that. I just meant we didn't want to inconvenience you more than we already had."

"Oh, okay, then. Well, what do you want to ask them about that day?" He continued to stand proud with a strong willed tone.

"We want to know about that day, when the preacher was shot in the middle of the street you reside on. What did they see? Who did they see?"

"Well, I can cut straight to the chase with that. I already asked them about that day, but if you like, I will do it again. Abdul and Fatima, did you see anyone kill anyone?" The father looked his children dead in the eye. "Be honest. Do not lie to this man. Allah is watching you and sees all. Do not be punished in paradise for lying."

Remembering the various times the mean-spirited, ulterior-motive preacher threatened to tell their father on them, the brother and sister made a pact. They had jointly agreed to keep their mouths shut, knowing Allah would forgive them for the lie in the long run. "No, sir, not at all," the older one spoke for them both, also remembering Clay saving them from being bullied. "We were still at the store. When we came back, the man from the church was lying there, in the middle of the street. Dad, we didn't stop, I swear. We just kept coming straight home and in the house like you tell us to always do. The only time I looked out the window was when the news cameras were there and the ambulance."

"Do both of you swear on this Holy Quran," he asked, holding the sacred book outward for his children to see.

"Yes, Dad, I swear," Abdul swiftly replied as the detectives looked on.

"Yes, Daddy," Fatima chimed in, following her big brother's lead.

"Okay, well, there you have it. They have sworn on Allah, and there is no greater judge than that!" The father held his head high. He was a man of strong faith and believed in his children. Waiting for any opposition to his statement or that of his offspring, he asked once more, "Now, is that all you need to ask of them, or do I have to get a lawyer? We have evening prayers to attend at the mosque."

The detective lowered his head in defeat. He knew it was useless to push this any further—that was, unless he wanted to start a mini jihad at the station. "No, sir, that's all at this time. Once again, sorry for the inconvenience, but keep in mind, we may still be in touch at a later day."

After that explosive exchange, the man and his children stepped back on the elevator. There was no more conversation or questioning to take place. The man and his children were all stone-faced mean mugging until the door slid shut.

"Son of a bitch! This shit is crazy. We keep running into a brick wall with what should be an open-and-shut case. I don't know what to say or think. Maybe the information we received is wrong. It seems like these people don't know anything, or all of them are putting on a good act. But why would they protect an animal like that fool we got locked up? It's baffling. They may just have the crazy misfortune of living on the block the reverend was killed on . . . nothing more, nothing less."

The other detective smirked. "Yeah, maybe in a perfect world, but this is freaking Detroit. Life ain't that simple here. Everybody watching your black ass even when you think they ain't. Now *somebody* saw something. We just gotta keep digging. One of these people on the list gonna flip on that asshole we got locked up. It's only a matter of time. Besides, even if we don't get an open charge of murder now, he's got a hellava lot of other bullshit we can dig up on him and make stick."

"Yeah, dude, that sounds good and all, but time is what we don't have. The clock is ticking before we charge up or cut loose. You know the reporters, the chief, and the mayor is on our asses like white on rice. We gotta shit or get off the pot on this one."

As if on cue, the other set of detectives on the team working the case emerged from the second interview room. Like their counterparts, they appeared to look disappointed as well. Going into the main office, they all sat down to compare notes. "Okay, so how did your interviews go with the teacher Lynn Banks and the two Arab kids?"

"Well, the teacher was a no-go. What she told us seemed to make good sense. She didn't appear to be rattled as if she was holding something back, but you never know in these cases, although she was annoyed we came to her job. But in truth, who wouldn't be pissed off if the damn police come snooping around your damn job?"

"Yeah, man, you right about that. I, for one, wouldn't want your ugly ass popping up asking my damn boss no shit about me," one detective tried his best to lighten the otherwise grim mood in the room.

"Yeah, very funny, dude. You a regular Bernie Mac. But yeah, and as for the kids, first of all, they are black *not* Arab."

"Damn, my bad," the detective looked down at his notes which had a list of the potential witnesses. "I just assumed when I saw the names . . ."

"Yeah, well, guy, they are black. And their father is black too—all the way fucking black. Shit, as black as a nigga can get and militant as hell." He laughed looking at his partner to back him up, who did by laughing as well. "Straight off the Million Man March black! But the kids were solid. Neither one blinked an eye; even the little girl was a soldier. I mean, if they did see something that damn day, their father got them so terrified of his wrath they'd tell us who killed King, JFK, and where Jimmy Hoffa was buried at. He's one of them fathers that have zero tolerance about going against what he says."

Sharing a laugh, the other team revealed their updates with the two persons or interest they had spoken to. "Well, I just got finished talking to the old woman, a Mrs. Thelma Gale." He searched through the papers in his hand so he could give his colleagues an accurate account of what was said. "Mrs. Gale was picked up by one of the officers downstairs. She doesn't drive so, of course, we took care of that. So to get down to the real business, I asked her did she know Reverend Richards well."

"And what was her response, because the three folk we spoke to act as if they didn't even know the man's name for sure?" the lead from the first team interjected.

"She said of course she knew him. Matter of fact, she said she'd known him for some years. He'd been in her house, and she'd been at his church ever since he first took over."

Anxiousness filled the room in anticipation that they finally had caught a real true break in the case. On pins and needles, the two initial detectives waited. All four of their jobs were on the line, so Mrs. Gale's statement had the prospective to be gold. Hopefully, her statement would be the nail in Clay's coffin.

"Okay, guy, go ahead, bring it home for us all! We're waiting for the slam dunk! We need this break, so come on and be the hero."

"Hold up now. Pump your damn breaks. Don't start the celebration yet. Well, as she knows him or rather knew him, she claim ain't see nothing. She said it was pretty much a wrap for the preacher by the time she got to her front window."

"Aww, damn, her front window? The tip said she, like all the rest of the supposed witnesses, were there, shoulder to shoulder with our victim and perp when the shit popped off. Now here's another one that wasn't really there. What in the hell was going on that day on that damn block? Was everyone temporary blind or some shit like that? Or was that tip some straight up bullshit?"

"Listen, she told me she was taking her high blood pressure medicine. And then when she was testing her sugar level she heard a few gunshots. She said hearing them had become normal around there, so she didn't bother to think twice about it. However, she claims when she finally did get to her front window, she looked out. She said she wasn't 100 percent sure, but she thought she'd seen what appeared to be someone lying in the street. The old woman said she had to go back and get her glasses off the dining room table where she had been sitting to make out who it was. And if you would've seen the way she moves, that took another damn ten minutes to get back over to that damn window."

"Wow, okay, then what?" one detective asked the other, wishing he would speed the statement up.

"Well, she said she saw her longtime friend Reverend Richards. She said he was sprawled out on the curb and heard the sounds of police sirens coming. That's why she claims she didn't call 911. She said she just stood there in the window and prayed he was all right. She said she was much too scared to open her front door, let alone go outside. She just stood there and looked."

"Well, okay. Please tell us, did she see anyone else out there? Please tell me she said yes," the elder of all the four detectives eagerly questioned. "I'm too old to be demoted to a school crossing guard if we don't solve this case. Hell, I'ma need to take my damn blood pressure meds too just like the old woman."

"Naw, man, she didn't see anything I can gather that would be considered a home run. Just a couple of kids she thinks, like off toward the far end of the block. Like maybe they were coming from the store or something like that. Now she might be lying, but I wasn't gonna push her. She had a damn Bible with her in one hand and could hardly talk without quoting scriptures. Plus had two canes with her, for God's sake." He shrugged his shoulders in disappointment of letting the team down. "I think she's a definite no all across the board in being concrete as far as witnesses go."

"Damn! Well, truth be told, that matches with what I have here after talking to them Muslim kids and their radical-power-to-the-people-ass father. So I guess the old lady was being truthful." He shook his head feeling like they were running into a dead end in the high-profile case. "And that schoolteacher wasn't even on the damn block—or at least so she says."

"Fuck! This is way beyond crazy! A man dies, gunned down, murdered in broad daylight—and no one sees any-damn-thing. I mean, we both know Clay Jennings had every reason to kill the man, but thinking it and proving it is far, few, and in between. We need some hard-core facts and some eyewitnesses putting him at the scene. I mean, damn, we don't even have a murder weapon. This is adding up to be some real Class-A bull-shit in the making."

"Well, according to that anonymous tip that initially came in fingering Clay Jennings as the shooter, we should have a slam dunk with Mr. and Mrs. Jessie when they come in tomorrow. From what we know from Reverend Richards's brother, he is the Block Club president and was a close confidant of the preacher. He has to know something. Hell, he may be our final shot."

"Okay, good—good. Let's hope so, because the young girl Trinity Walker that was also supposed to be there when the crime took place is, nine outta ten times, a definite no-go as well. Just by talking to her on her front stairs of her house this morning, she made it perfectly clear she was, as she put it . . . 'to busy sucking her man's dick' to be concerned with whatever went on way down the street from her bedroom."

"Say *what* now? Are you for real?" The other cops jointly laughed at what they'd just heard.

"Come on now. You can't really be serious," another said.

"Yeah, the hell I am. I stood there trying to question her about this and that, and either she is a great actress or just dumb as a bag of rocks. Just like the rest of these young females out here, she got a one-track mind on sex, drugs, and more damn sex. And by the way, she was making sure I saw she didn't have any panties on underneath her criminally short skirt. I believe the little hood rat was ready to go right there on her front stairs. If she wasn't busy sucking some fool off that day our victim was killed, she should've been. So, yeah, like I said, we must have been ill advised with her. She's a definite no-go as an eyewitness. Hell, she needs to be at someone's charm school. The girl is out of control, like most of these young folk in Detroit."

Chapter Twenty-five

Lynn Banks

Lynn's throat was bone dry. She had one of the most severe headaches ever. *Lord, help me!* Pressing the palm of her left hand to her forehead and her right to her heart, her eyes grew watery. Not being able to function regularly without her morning blast, the distraught teacher leaned against the wall of a building. Hoping she had dodged the bullet of suspicion, her mind was all over the place. Her eyes darted from side to side. The once-teacher-of-the-year was paranoid, thinking she was being followed and the entire world was focused on watching her every move. Emotionally drained from what she had seen take place on the block, she was at her breaking point. *Oh my God. I hope they believe me. Oh my God. I can't breathe. I think I'm gonna pass out right here in the middle of the street. Jesus, help me.*

Ms. Banks endured what seemed like hours of grueling, brow-beating questioning pertaining to the day Reverend Richards was murdered. Although she had stood mute as the cold-blooded killing took place, there was no way in the name of sweet baby Jesus that she would admit to that feat. It wasn't that the educator didn't have any remorseful feelings about seeing a man take his last breath; it was the fact she couldn't risk losing her job. If the detectives found out the true reason for her being on the block, her life would be over. She'd lose everything.

Besides her own selfish motives, placing the blame of the horrific crime on Clay would make her a fraud. In reality, she'd gotten down on her knees the night prior asking God to remove the threat-filled corrupt preacher from her life. Truth be told, she was glad he was dead and gone and wanted nothing more than to reward Clay for the act. As she drove off in search of a few rocks of crack to get her out the gate, Lynn Banks looked back over at the police station and said a silent prayer Clay would beat the case and most importantly, no one else out there that day could identify her.

The Silah Family

Mr. Silah was fuming as he stepped foot off the elevator. With his offspring trailing close behind, he shook his head in defiance. Visibly upset with the system, the devout Muslim loudly let each officer that was on front-desk duty know just that. He felt slighted. He felt as if the detectives obviously had no real leads and were grasping at straws. It was bad enough the police had the nerve to send a squad car with flashing lights to his home as if *his* children had committed the crime themselves. They'd endangered his family, possibly having them labeled as snitches in the drug-infested neighborhood. Now, here they had added insult to injury. Now the "slimeball" as he referred to them detectives, had grilled his children repeatedly about what they'd seen the day the so-called Christian man of the cloth was killed. Mr. Silah knew his children. He trusted his children. He believed in his children. And most importantly, the father knew that his children would not lie to him or in the name of Allah.

Voicing his opinion, he let it be known he resented the implication from the officers that his teenage son, Abdul, and his baby girl would deceive them when it came to an act as serious as murder. The strict Muslim father practically dragged Fatima by her small arm as he marched the children toward the family car. Ignoring the stares and judgmental whispers of how they were dressed, he vowed to file several complaints. "They can't treat us like this. It's because we are black and because we follow Islam. Well, I'm gonna have justice served against them one day soon. This is not over by a long shot." As he drove off into traffic, he glanced back over his shoulder at both children. Seeing them stare out the rear window, he could only wonder what was truly on both their minds.

Once home, Abdul and Fatima were asked to go to their rooms so their parents could discuss what had taken place at the police department. Making sure the door was closed, the two children could finally exhale and let their guard down.

"Big brother, I was scared. I almost told them the truth."

"Don't worry. You did good, Fatima. I was proud of you, okay? They believed us, and Daddy believed us too."

"Yeah, I know, but we swore in front of the Quran. We lied, and now we gonna burn in hellfire later."

"No, we are not. Dad always just tells us that to try to scare us. Allah knows our true heart and knows why we had to stay silent. That man Reverend Richards was bad and evil. And Clay always helped us when we needed it. We had to try to help him too."

"Abdul, I know, he always helps us. But who is going to help us now if he's in jail?"

"That's what I'm talking about. That's why we had to keep our mouths shut. If we would have said something, we would have been helping get him in trouble even more. And we couldn't do that to our friend. Now, you understand that, don't you?"

"Yes," she simply replied.

"Then let's just pray for Clay's freedom and ourselves to stay strong."

Trinity Walker

Trinity tightly held the gold chain with a diamond-encrusted cross, the one that once belonged to Reverend Bernard Richards before his untimely demise. When Clay snatched if off the crooked preacher's neck and allowed it to drop to the ground, she snatched it up. Quickly realizing Clay's fingerprints were on the expensive piece of jewelry, Trinity didn't want it to fall into the wrong hands. She knew the shade was real on the block. She had felt it when Rhonda and her friends attacked her and no one stepped up in her defense except for Clay. And she also felt it when she and her kids were in line at the church waiting for a free food box. So, of course, it was safe to assume there were more than a few people standing out in the streets with her that day who were self-righteous. Trinity definitely didn't know if their intentions were pure as far as Clay was concerned, so she did what had to be done. And the young mother of two knew the chances of them doing what she had done earlier were slim to none.

Standing tall when the detective came knocking at her front door, she knew what had to be done. Clay had come to her rescue on more than a few occasions, so it was the least she could do to return the favor. Although there were plenty of witnesses to the brazen murder Clay had committed, Trinity wasn't going to be the one weak link. There was no way in hell she would go down in long-term memory hood history as a rat or snitch. Besides, in her heart of hearts, she wished she had the balls to do what Clay had done. Reverend Richards had taken advantage of her countless times in various forms. He'd talked to her like she was no more than a piece of shit on his shoe and threaten to call Child Protective Services when he could not get his way. The fact that she stood idly by watching him beg for mercy was enough to make her come in her own panties. Trinity found solace in knowing the crooked, out-for-himself preacher deserved everything he had coming—and more. There was definitely a place in hell waiting for him.

Fuck that ho-ass nigga. I hope he rot. I should have spit in his face one good time before he died. Old fake-ass pussy. Trinity had been in her feelings just like that as the police detective knocked at the door. After peeking out the curtain and realizing who it was, she knew she had to come through. Not only for herself to avoid the cops thinking she knew or had saw jack shit that day, but to come through for Clay as well. He deserved her loyalty and was going to get just that.

After swinging the door wide open, she went into action. The young mother made sure the wide-eyed detective could easily see everything she was working with. Just falling short of parting her legs and inviting him to dive in, Trinity played the role of the neighborhood slut. Without much effort of explaining where she was that afternoon in question, she made it clear she was busy doing what she did best—fuck and suck dick for sport and gain. The detective was not only convinced of her whereabouts and actions, but seconds away from being snatched into her sexually charged web himself. When Ms. Walker finally took his card promising to call if she heard anything in the streets, the detective was dry mouthed, ready to go home and take a cold shower.

I ain't gonna be the one to fold Clay. I swear I got you until the wheels fall off. Ain't no nigga or bitch gonna make me turn my back on you after all the times you done held me down. Trinity thought about going to sell the chain at the pawn shop and give the money to Clay to help if he needed a lawyer but knew the police would maybe trace the deceased monster's property back to her. Instead, she chilled and watched the block to see who was doing what. She'd taken notice that squad cars had been in front of the old woman's apartment as well as the Muslim family's house. The only thing Trinity could do was pray they had not said shit either. But she knew others around there were not cut like her.

Mrs. Gale

"Thank you so much for the ride. I showl appreciate you young men, but like I told the detectives, I didn't see anything." Against every rule she'd ever taught her children growing up, she lied.

"No problem. We understand, Mrs. Gale. And it was no problem at all," one of the officers smiled as he pulled up in front of the place Mrs. Gale called home. "We definitely appreciate you as well. We don't expect every day to be Christmas or New Year's Eve. Sometimes we may strike out," he nonchalantly announced as he wasn't a detective, just a uniformed driver.

"I know, but I feel bad for you all to go through all of this trouble, and I could not help you." She reached for her cane and purse as the other officer opened her door. "All of this fuss for nothing. But it was a nice ride, though. And he is a real good driver."

Now out of the rear seat of the squad car, she hoped they bought all the tall tales she had told in the name of protecting Clay. Mrs. Gale's shaky hands held tightly onto the black metal safety rail. Each step she took was one of guilt and shame, but still, she knew she did what she had to do for the young man that had shown her so much compassion over the past month or so. *I pray Clay is doing okay. I wish I could talk to him or at least lay eyes on him.*

With a snail's pace, she made her way up her front stairs. As Mrs. Gale stood at the top landing of the porch of the apartment building, the elderly woman watched the police car roar down the road. Attempting to catch her breath, she took her time to look up and down the street. *Oh my goodness. It's like I'm in a dream. I need to go upstairs and get my Bible.* This was the same block she had lived on for years. Sadly, this was the first time in quite a while the block was as motionless as it was. Mrs. Gale saw no drug dealers, no crackheads waiting in line to be served, and no people in need milling about in hopes of receiving food assistance boxes. The senior citizen didn't even see her longtime neighbors, Mr. and Mrs. Jessie, out and about.

Once upstairs, Thelma sat down in her favorite chair. Reaching for her Bible, she began to read scriptures. Caught up in her thoughts, she began to think more about Clay. Her mind wandered and wished he was born kin to her. She knew that if that had been the case, maybe she could have stepped into his turbulent life years before the present. Maybe, just maybe, Clay would have been able to finish school and pursue a career other than that of a drug dealer and murderer. At various points during their impromptu conversations, Mrs. Gale easily saw glimpses of his other side; the good, God-fearing side that wanted no more than to do right. Clay's inner soul seemed to be begging to be saved. Mrs. Gale felt all she needed was more time to do so.

As she held the Bible open reading, she rocked her body back and forth. Removing her glasses, tears started to form in the corner of her weary eyes. *My, my, my.*

Why did you have to do it, Clay? Why? I knew Reverend Richards was no good. He did things that no man of God should have even participated in, and he definitely deserved to be held to task for all his sins. And maybe I should have stood up a long time ago and said something about what things I saw and knew were taking place in that wicked house of worship. Lord have mercy. I'm so sorry I failed you, boy. Oh, my sweet child, Clay. You deserve so much better than what the rest of your life holds. You deserve not to be locked up. But you is. You is, and I can't do nothing to help you; nothing but pray. And I know I can't turn back the hands of time.

Mrs. Gale placed her Bible down on the end table and struggled to stand. Making her way over to the front window, she moved the sheer curtain over to the side. Regretfully, she then peered out. The block was still quiet, as if it knew its fearless leader was doomed. Taking a hold of her feelings, her eyes focused as best they could. She looked upon the very spot where the crime of what would certainly be considered cold-blooded murder had taken place. The one and same place she saw her pastor take a few slugs to the body, then take his final breaths. *I know you are truly guilty of what the police was asking me about down at that place, but I just could not bear to be the one to assist them in your demise. I know other people was standing out there. And I am more than sure they don't know you like I think I do, so let them tell the tale. The fact that I lied, I know God will forgive me. And you know what, Clay? If you repent, he will forgive you as well.*

Preoccupied with everything going on with the young man who she'd adopted into her heart, Mrs. Gale had failed to constantly call her own biological children. Even when the news of Reverend Richards's murder was plastered all across the papers and television screens, her kids had also failed to get in touch with their mother. She was content knowing Clay, and she had formed the bond that they had. Thelma Gale went back to sit down, hoping her little friend knew.

Chapter Twenty-six

The Cops

"Okay, this is looking like our only chance to wrap this shit up and save face. I have a strong feeling in my gut these two are gonna bury that murdering son of a bitch we got locked up. And if they do, we can finally go home to our families and get some rest."

"Let's pray for your sake and mine," the lead homicide detective told his partner, making sure he had a pad and pen ready, "because in between the chief, the mayor, and all the damn reporters, our necks are on the line here. This is the most terrible case I've ever had the misfortune to catch. At first, I thought it would be simple one, two, three."

"You telling me," his partner agreed, holding up a memo that just came in from the Prosecutor's Office as well. "I ain't trying to have no unsolved mark on this case. They up there in the higher-up's office talking about demoting all our asses. Fuck that. I'll take an early retirement first."

After a few more minutes of chatter about how the case was going and how badly they needed a home run, the final witnesses arrived.

"Hello, everyone," Mr. Jessie spoke as he and his wife walked through the squad room door.

"Yes, hello. Come on in and please have a seat. Mr. and Mrs. Jessie, correct?"

"Yes, indeed. I trust we are on time?"

"Yes, you are on time, and we definitely appreciate that. Can we get you two anything . . . coffee, tea, maybe a bottled water?" the detective asked as only a formality, as he was ready to get down to the pressing business at hand.

"No, thank you," Mrs. Jessie answered for them both. "We just finished with our breakfast, so we're good."

"Okay, then, let's just get to it, shall we?"

"Of course. By all means, go ahead." Mr. Jessie's heart was racing inside, but he sat perfectly still. "How can my wife and I help?"

"Well, first of all, before we get started," the detective watched for any signs of nervousness but saw none, "me and my partner want to say sorry for your loss. We understand you and the victim were close. Is that true?"

"Yes, it is. I mean, you can say that," Mr. Jessie replied as he looked over toward the window, wishing he could just fly away like one of the birds that was sitting on the ledge.

"Well, hopefully, you can help us put away the monster that committed the crime," the detective said, folding back the first sheet of the yellow legal pad. He questioned Mrs. Jessie first. "So, can you tell us where exactly you were when Bernard Richards was murdered?"

"Well, I was working in my garden in the backyard, and my husband was getting me a bag of top soil out of the garage. The rosebush was needing a little bit of reinforcements. The strong rains and wind the other week had it bending over some."

"Okay, is this true," the detective then questioned Mr. Jessie as he wrote down every single word Mrs. Jessie had said, "you were in the rear of your dwelling . . . in the garage like your wife said?"

"Of course it is, young man. What are you trying to say?"

"Nothing, sir—nothing at all. Just trying to get both your statements correct, that's it." He tried to hold his composure, hoping this interview wasn't headed in the same direction as all the others had gone. "I mean, a man gets murdered directly in front of your home, you are both yards away, and didn't see it? That's strange."

"Listen, Officer," Mrs. Jessie hastily intervened, sensing her husband might break under pressure, "the neighborhood we live in has changed so very much over the previous years. It used to be families that care about each other. We used to all go on picnics and vacations together. But all of that has since changed. My husband does the best he can, but sometimes, it's not good enough. It's like he is a one-man army. So, you see, on our block, you liable to hear arguing, loud noises, and gunfire, morning, noon, and night."

The detective could hardly keep up with everything she was saying, so he stopped trying to write and just listened. "I understand you and your husband's plight, I truly do."

"Okay, well, as I was saying, so when we heard the gunshot, we ran back in our rear door and locked it. It sounded so close, there was no way in Jesus' name we were going to just stand there in the backyard, let alone run to investigate. We just ran inside and prayed whoever was shooting didn't come our way."

"My wife is right. We took cover like we've been doing for years now since we have no real police presence over there. I try my best to watch and see what's going on, but it's hard. It's just so rough over there." Mr. Jessie pulled it together a lot quicker than he did the night they got robbed, even trying to flip the script on the inquisitive cops. "Like she said, the shots were so loud; extremely loud. It wasn't until we felt it was safe that I finally opened the front door and saw my friend lying on the ground bleeding."

"Well, did either of you call 911?"

"Umm, no, I guess I was in shock," he quickly replied. "I wasn't expecting to see him there. I mean, he and I had shared some pretty decent times over the years. We had common goals and interests. We both wanted to see the block regain its beauty and unity. We both knew it was a long shot, but we believed in the dream."

"I was going to call 911, but before we knew it, the police and ambulance were there. I mean, it all happened so quick; there was nothing either one of us could do but pray." Thankful for Clay saving her and her husband from those young predators, there would be no way whatsoever they would betray him, especially for someone like the unscrupulous, self-serving Reverend Richards had become. It was as if she had traded one block tormentor for the next, but nothing was more important than her husband's freedom. Standing by Clay was an easy choice to make.

"Well, at least, did you see anyone or recognize any voices?" the other detective in the office eagerly asked.

"Sorry, no. Like my wife said, we were in the backyard when we heard the gunshots." Mr. Jessie held the same exact attitude as his spouse when it came to delivering Clay's fate on a silver platter. "Then we rushed in the house, making sure to stay there until whatever was happening was over."

Regretful, seeing their sure-fire witnesses had gone from sugar to shit, the detectives informed the couple they could leave, but the department would be in touch if they had any further questions. They walked Mr. and Mrs. Jessie to the elevator, and when the door closed, they felt their last hopes of bringing a swift end to this high-profile murder was over.

"Ain't this about some crazy and wild bullshit? That damn caller said it was seven motherfucking people out in the street standing around watching that man get done in cold blood, and they all supposedly ain't see jack shit. I don't understand it. Hell, they all act like they don't even know Clay Jennings, even though he's been slinging dope on their block for some time now. But I'm not crazy. I know how street life goes. You see, but you don't see. You hear, but you don't hear. Me and my family was once held captive by that mentality, but it kept us alive and out of harm's way until we could relocate and do better. So even though I don't like the game these people probably playing when it comes to snitching, I can relate. But damn, I still don't know how they can act like Clay is a stranger altogether."

"Me either." Holding the memo, the detective grew infuriated coming up empty-handed on pressing first-degree homicide charges on Clay Jennings—their only suspect. "I mean, I can see the young ratchet female and possibly the kids being with that no-snitching crap, maybe. But a goddamn schoolteacher, an old lady, and now these two? The shit don't make no damn sense." He walked over to the window staring across the Detroit skyline. "I can't figure this thing out. Seven different people from all different walks of life covering up for that thug don't compute with me. What's the connection?"

"Man, at this point, it don't matter." The lead detective stood to his feet looking for the keys to the holding cells. "That buster's overpriced lawyer is all over this bullshit, and the memo from the prosecutor said if we don't have a witness by one or maybe two p.m., we gotta cut him loose."

Mr. and Mrs. Jessie

"Sweetheart, trust me when I tell you we did the right thing. Don't worry. We did a great job of covering it up."

Accepting the reassuring rub on the shoulder his wife was giving him, Mr. Jessie exhaled. In all his years of living, he had never once experienced anything like he'd just gone through over the past week or so. One minute his life was what he deemed as normal. He would wake up, maybe run his wife to the store. Then tend to some yard work and keep a watchful eye on what the brazen drug dealers were doing across from the longtime place he called home. Now, here they were leaving the police department after talking to homicide detectives. "Honey, are you sure that they bought it? I was extremely nervous. Matter of fact, I think I stumbled a few times."

Mrs. Jessie clutched her purse close to her chest as they walked, praying what she was telling her husband was true. Finally, they got into the car. "Look, we did what we had to do. And we said what we had to say just now. That boy might be a drug dealer, but he stepped up, stepped in, and saved us both that night. You and I both know we could be dead if it wasn't for him. Those little monsters tore up our house and disrespected me. I was terrified when you left with that thug. I was in the closet praying, not knowing if I would live to see another day."

"Yes, that's true, dear." Mr. Jessie started the engine.

"Now, whereas I don't agree with, by no means at all, what he did out in the street to Reverend Richards, the man had it coming, and we had no other choice but to cover up our own sins. I couldn't stand the thought of you being in that boy's spot. Think about it. It was by your hand that the monster in the backyard is gone. We have to respect what he is locked up in there for doing by keeping his mouth shut."

"Once again, you're right. He could throw us, well, me, anyways, underneath the bus," Mr. Jessie said as he pulled off into traffic. "But obviously, that's not his intention. I guess he's a lot more than just some gangbanging drug dealer. And as heinous as the act of what he did to Reverend Richards, who am I to judge?"

In total agreement, they would sell their house and relocate. The block they had called home and the house they'd raised their son in was tainted. Living there after the violation of the out of control teens would be too much. As they turned on their street, Mr. and Mrs. Jessie prayed them not bearing witness against Clay would aid him in being set free. Although considering all the other people who were on the block that fateful day, they knew the possibility of that taking place was probably slim to none. They vowed to never forget Clay and to always make sure to keep money on his books when he went to prison . . . of course, anonymously.

Chapter Twenty-seven

The Lawyer

After being led back to the out-of-the-way one-man cell, the highly paid lawyer of Clay Jennings was infuriated. First, at the fact he'd been treated as if he himself murdered someone as he was roughly frisked; second, that he was being made to meet and speak with his client under these circumstances; and last, that Clay was being held so long without being formally charged with any crime.

"Don't worry," he fumed as he struggled to write on his canary-yellow legal pad while standing outside the locked cell, "by the time I'm done with these cops and the inhumane way you and I are both being treated, we will have all their pensions by the balls. This type of thing is extremely irregular and uncalled for."

Clay was glad he'd kept up on all the cash he'd paid to have a legal mouthpiece on call 24/7. He was sure that if nothing else, his civil rights would be protected. However, he stood mute when the lawyer revealed what he claimed the detectives had in tow when speaking with them.

"Now, son, I ain't gonna lie to you. That ain't gonna make shit any easier for you to swallow and me to deal with. Now, going under the assumption that what they say they have is indeed truth, we will be definitely fighting an uphill battle."

"Okay, then, don't hold me up. What they ho asses claim?" Clay asked, already knowing it was a loaded question. "What they got so crucial that's gonna be a surprise to me?"

The lawyer turned the page on the pad and scribbled down a few more notes while fact checking some others. "Well, low key, one of the detectives I've dealt with before claims this is going to be one of the easiest slam dunks ever. He says they have a slew of eyewitnesses just about lining up to take their turn to testify against you. The man claims while you're looking at a case of open murder now, by nightfall, it will be amped up to possibly first degree on every single body they have found, not just that preacher. I heard they are getting desperate as the hours go by."

"Oh yeah? Ain't that some shit? Man, fuck that ho-ass Bible-carrying fraud. He had it coming. I swear I wish I could get out and kill the son of a bitch all the way the fuck over again!"

Quick to silence his boisterous client, the lawyer looked around for any prying eyes or ears. "Look-a here, Clay, you gotta stop all that talking you doing right now. Be cool. Stay calm. Now like I said, it's definitely gonna be one for the books if the cops have what they say they have and we walk away without getting football numbers. But anything is possible. Just stay the hell calm and let me do my job. In the meantime, I'm gonna work on getting you either charged so we can get on with the get-on or cut loose. I already paid the bail and got them to release your two friends, so they good. They're free. Now, for the detectives who claim to have all these fabulous firecracker eyewitnesses, it's about to be show and proof time on your behalf."

Clay stood tall. With a mean mug, he walked away from the heavy steel bars and sat on his bunk. He had no remorse for doing what he had to do. Reverend Richards was a rat; nothing more and nothing less. And if everyone had to get a firsthand account of what happened to rats in the streets, so be it. It was what it was and what would be would be.

Rhonda

"I see both y'all crazy busters got outta that mother-fucker hell trap, huh?" she smiled as Whip walked over, kissing her on the lips.

"Damn. What in the fuck kinda slimeball bullshit is y'all on?" Dorie shockingly asked taking two steps backward. "What's up with all that? Y'all got a nigga confused as hell."

"Come on, dawg, like I told you when we was locked up in there dude, fuck Clay. That sucker straight is over. He 'bout to do life for that crazy shit he pulled in broad daylight. I seen that shit all over the news, plus all the detectives been on our ass. You already know the way they was pressing us; he gonna do life for killing that preacher. That dumb-ass, bright-skin pussy nigga better be lucky we ain't got the death penalty here in Michigan."

"Yeah," Rhonda quickly interjected, "because if they did, his ass would have a poison-filled needle dangling in his arm. His cheating ass would be in the morgue by daybreak."

Dorie couldn't believe what he was seeing and hearing. With dirty clothes on his back and smelling like a few foul nights in the county jail, he wanted nothing more than to take a hot shower and brush his teeth. However, Whip and Rhonda were obviously showing their true colors toward Clay, taking center stage, so he waited. "Dawg, that guy sent us both a fucking lawyer and paid our bail before he got knocked, and now you out here throwing

dirt on his name just like that? That's foul," Dorie cam-
paigned for his homeboy, not ready to accept half of what
could be factual. Clay was about to do some serious time
for murdering the preacher in front of all the witnesses
the detectives had bragged to them about having. "And
all that shit them ho-ass police saying he did on the
block as far as us being is some bullshit too. Clay been a
hundred with us from jump street, flat the fuck out. So
y'all can miss me with the rest of that madness."

"Fuck Clay. Fuck his devious wanna-fuck-everything-
that-move ass—like he king of Detroit," Rhonda fumed
as she kissed Whip once more on the mouth. "My new
man Whip is right. He about to come up in the game and
take his rightful spot, and I'm gonna be right by his side,
posted. Clay is over in these streets. It's Whip's day."

"Yo, y'all both truly bugging." Dorie didn't want any
part of what they were conspiring on against his people.
"So this that new so-called bad bitch you been fucking
around with that was so top secret? Damn. You creep
foul for this one for sure!"

"What's that supposed to mean?" Rhonda planted both
hands on her hips and bucked her eyes.

"It means just what in the fuck it sounds like it means."
Dorie was far from backing down on how he felt. "You
two is on some real snake shit. I expect that from your
hood rat in a skirt ass desperate for a come up. But, Whip,
come on, dawg, don't go out on our people like this;
especially with a ho like this riding shotgun."

"Fuck Clay," Whip yelled out toward the jail, hoping
Clay could hear him through the concrete walls and
paint-darkened windows. "Ole boy was conveniently not
there when the shit jumped and changed his number—
like fuck us. So guess what? It's fuck him."

"Yeah, so it's fuck Clay. I already told you once—Clay is
done," Rhonda bragged with a smile on her face, tugging

down on her skintight fitted shirt. "I made sure of that when I called the police on his good lying sneaky ass! Killing that man in front of all them people like they about that street life and gonna ride for him. They done rounded up and got all them good, law-abiding citizens who seen him do it. So you already know his reckless ass fucked in the game now fo'sho." Rhonda bitterly frowned, showing every jealous bone in her body. "Now let that slut Trinity he cares so much about protecting go hold him down in jail for the rest of his life! Fuck 'em both!"

Dorie was disgusted. He couldn't believe Whip. This was pissing him all the way off. It was bad enough the cops had him up every hour on the hour trying to get some information about their operations. But now this. It was only a few short forty-eight hours or so ago that he, Whip, and Clay were getting money and living like hood kingpins. Walking away from his newly former friend and his rat-ass-mentality new bitch, Dorie started walking toward the hood after calling for a ride. Clay may have been facing life after killing ole boy in broad daylight, but there was no way in hell he was gonna just be flat-out disrespectful, considering all they'd been through over the years. "Stand tall, my dude. You got this. Linwood for life." Dorie spit on the ground as Rhonda and Whip sped by with smiles on both their faces.

Chapter Twenty-eight

The Aftermath

"Well, this is it. We gotta let this bastard free. As much as we hate it, it looks like he done messed around and got away with murder. We done pressed all those witnesses and put our foot on his workers' necks when we had them locked up. Still no damn cigar. This son of a bitch gotta be one of the luckiest motherfuckers alive."

"Yeah, this time, maybe. But a guy with as much on his rap sheet as Clay Jennings has, he'll be back. This time he just dodged the bullet. But before we give up totally, I want to at least place a call to each of the fraudulent witnesses and see if they remember something else or have had some sort of miraculous change of heart since last contact with us." With a hopeful spirit, he then sat down behind his paper-scattered desk and started the task. First on his list was the teacher, Lynn Banks. Forced to leave a voice mail, she eventually returned the call after school hours. She stuck to her story and asked not to be bothered any further. Next, the detective reluctantly dialed Mr. Silah's number. After two rings, he picked up and wasted no time in vowing to lawyer up and bring racial and religious harassment suits against the entire Detroit Police Department if they continued to make an issue about what his children "didn't see." The detective knew he wanted to avoid any extra dealings with the chief and mayor should a lawsuit be involved, so he ended the conversation as quickly as possible, being as apologetic for the intrusions as he could be. Shaking his head, he knew he had to at least give it a shot, and he'd done just that. He felt there was no great need to get in touch with the Trinity Walker or Mrs. Gale, but just as he forced himself to call Mr. Silah, he proceeded to do the same with them as well. Mrs. Gale answered almost immediately. To the detective's credit, he allowed her to damn near talk his ear off about God this and God that before telling her thank you for your time after finally hearing she knew nothing else more than what she'd originally revealed. Speaking to Trinity made him damn near sick to his stomach the way she cursed him out about calling her phone and told him to basically suck her dick, as if she really had one. He knew after that, it was time for him to retire and be on a boat somewhere fishing instead of being subjected to all that verbal abuse. Thankfully, Mrs. Jessie was more pleasant when reached. Although making it clear she and her husband could shed no further light on the untimely murder of Reverend Richards, she promised to call them if they happened to hear or see anything on the block that could assist in them closing the case and bringing closure to the victim's family.

"Well, I be damned. All seven of them done stood strong on their stories. I guess that tip we thought was the fucking bomb was no more than a damn dud. Shit. I'm running out of leads." The detective lowered his head in defeat, knowing he had to break the bad news to his team, and then, worst of all, the chief of police.

***

"Whelp, this is it. We ain't got no damn choice. We done grilled every witness, kept our foot on the necks of his homeboys, and ran behind every lead we got. Ain't shit left for us to do. This shit is messed up. I mean, who in the hell gets away with gunning down a well-known, respected, and loved preacher in the middle of the street and walks free? I mean, this arrogant punk done beat the damn system! I know it happens from time to time, but why on *my* damn watch?"

This was it. All the days of investigating, pounding the pavement, and taking crap from random citizens as far as the Richards's murder investigation was done. Over. Finished. It was looking as if it was final. The group of seasoned veteran detectives had shot their shot and failed miserably. As two of the weary minded and defeated detectives unlocked the main secured door, they looked at each other, shrugging their shoulders.

"Well, this shit didn't go as planned. Not at all."

"Naw, it really didn't. If you told me we'd be letting free the only possible shooter in this shameless case of murder, I would say you was crazy."

"Yup, I would say I was crazy too; but here the hell we is. I swear I hate this part in the job. The part where the bad guy thinks he won; thinks he beat the system."

"Yeah, man, me too. But it is what it is. Somebody gonna break one day, and if not him, then whoever truly murdered Reverend Richards will be brought to justice. It's only a matter of time. But for now, let's get on with it and cut this joker loose."

Full of regrets, they slowly approached the cell located all the way near the back of police headquarters. It was isolated from the others just in case the officers wanted to do or say things that were not deemed acceptable per the rules and regulations. The cell was no longer up to code, but it didn't matter. Although every cop on the force was not against bending the rules when need be, all felt that special prisoners accused of certain crimes deserved special treatment harsher than others. And all agreed Clay was one of those that deserve to be treated no better than shit on a stick.

With each step the detectives took, an eerie feeling came over them both. They momentarily made eye contact. Each felt as if something was wrong. It was extremely quiet. Clay Jennings was not one to hold his tongue. The suspected murderer with a rap sheet that was enormous was highly spirited, to say the least. Twice-convicted felon Clay had been loud, talking and cursing everyone out that would come within ten feet of his cell for what seemed like an eternity. Now the cops who he'd claim were trying to lock him away forever were only inches away, and the devout thug was silent as a church mouse.

Clay

"These ho-ass police done lost they minds. I swear if they think I'm gonna spend the rest of my life locked behind some bars on that no, sir, yes, sir, piss, eat, sleep, and take a dump when you tell me to bullshit, they wrong as fuck. Hell, naw. I'm tight on all that," Clay angrily reasoned out loud to himself. As he paced the small cell having just finished his jailhouse lunch tray, he knew his luck had run out. Not new to the game, he knew that no matter what the lawyer had said, his chances of seeing freedom again were slim to none. The

high-profile murder suspect was not just some average nigga out in the streets of Detroit with a nickel-and-
dime operation; he was known to have a real bag. And
unfortunately, Reverend Richards was not just an average, run-of-the-mill citizen. Clay bossed up, knowing
he'd done some real Wild-Wild West type of shit that
day on the block. The lawyer had informed him the
police claimed they had several eyewitnesses they knew
were solid and who were beating down the door to testify, so they had to be prepared for the fight of his life.
Clay came to grips that it was a no-win situation he'd
placed himself in and was not interested in giving the
cops, prosecutor, or judge the satisfaction of dragging
his good gangsta name through the mud. "I know damn
well outta all of them ham motherfuckers out there on
the block, the police gonna turn one of them, if not all."

Clay took off his shirt, tossing it onto the metal bunk.
Written on the wall, he saw the words "pray for me."
Immediately, he thought about the conversation he and
Mrs. Gale had about God and sinisterly grinned in denial.
"Yeah, where in the hell is God or Allah at now when a
nigga really need him? Damn some belief in something
you can't see. I'm out here by my lonesome as usual; an
army of one. Always was and always will be. When it
comes down to it—I got my own back. I ain't gonna let
nobody tell me how to do what I do. I'ma be OG with it all
the damn way."

Kicking off the brown-colored, jail-issued rubber flip-
flops, Clay then dropped his pants to the cold concrete
floor. He rubbed his bald head and thought about everything he'd been through over the years; his mother's
death, not knowing his father, wishing he had kids, and
how he had been a warrior through all his misfortunes.

Standing naked, he took a deep breath and got on to it. "Fuck prison and fuck the police! Can't no bars hold me back!"

"What the fuck! Shit! Damn! Damn!" The detective with the keys awkwardly fumbled, trying rapidly to unlock the heavy-duty steel bars. "Shit, this ain't good!"

"How in the hell? Quick, go call for medical help! Hurry up," the other one screamed out entering the small six-by-eight dimly lit cell. "This shit is messed up! Damn, hurry up, dude; call for a bus!"

In a mere matter of seconds, sheer pandemonium had jumped off. The detectives hated to have to face Clay and let him know that he had won for the time being, but this was a horse of a different color. They knew they had failed to make sure the deputies on duty checked in on Clay. They knew they would now catch the full-blown wrath of having him placed in the outdated cell in the first place. Yet, never in a million years did they think this could take place. Discovering a hood-driven rebellious Clay naked—swinging from the overhead ceiling fire sprinkler—eyes bucked wide open, the lead detective tried his best to cut the suspected killer down. In a desperate attempt to administer CPR, he practically beat on the prisoner's chest and used every breath in his own body in attempts to have Clay regain consciousness. Tragically, the detective soon found out it was too late. There was nothing he or the next man could do. All the medics, doctors, nurses, and ambulances together could not perform a jailhouse miracle. Clay's soul had made it all the way to heaven or hell. There was no turning back. Having had torn his jail uniform into rags and tying them together, Clay had made himself a makeshift noose. Determined not to spend the rest of his life caged up like a wild animal on featured display, he decided to save the taxpayers' money and take himself out of the game for good.

After his lawyer left delivering the grim state of the chances of his freedom, Clay's mind raced with what to do next. He swiftly realized he'd recently done a lot of wrong things, some for all the right reasons. It was not secret he would have undoubtedly had to have paid his debt to society. Indeed, he was guilty of cold-blooded murder, but he had become the exception to the rule due to the chain of events that'd taken place in the previous weeks. He'd made a true difference on the block and helped rid the world of Reverend Richards's reign of imposed righteousness. Unfortunately, the extremely seasoned criminal and self-proclaimed loner would never learn he was mere minutes away from beating the murder charge. It was just like Mrs. Gale told him, God shows up and shows out when you least expect him to. All Clay, seemingly born to be a throwaway, had to do was trust and believe in something greater than himself—a higher power.

Lying dead, Clay would never know all of the "supposed eyewitnesses" to his heinous act, who he thought would never ever have his back in a million years—in fact, did. Block Club activists Mr. and Mrs. Jessie, an overly religious Mrs. Gale, and Trinity, a party girl, all were on his team. The two kids that were scared of their own shadows, their father, and a drug-addicted schoolteacher, had, ironically, become an unbreakable stand-up group of a hard soldiers fighting for his freedom as well. There was absolutely no one willing to *testify* against him.

Whether it was their overwhelming "dislike and hate" for the seedy Reverend Richards or their appreciative "loyalty" to Clay Jennings, a ruthless killer, drug dealer, womanizer, and countless many other unsavory titles, the now-deceased young man would never know just what a difference he'd made in each of their lives.

The End